To Skies and Waters

Sirjan, as her name suggests, is a creative person. She expresses this creativity through her writing. She hails from a family of writers in Punjab. She has completed her bachelor's in Commerce from Hansraj College, University of Delhi, after which she has pursued a master's in Human Resources from the London School of Economics and Political Science. She has two books to her name: the first one is a book of poems titled *Whispers of the Heart*, and the second is a novel called *The Triumph*. Currently, she is working as People and Culture Manager in GFB Great Foods Pvt. Ltd.

E-mail: sirjansworld@gmail.com
Instagram: @sirjansworld

To
Skies
and
Waters

SIRJANDEEP KAUR UBHA

RUPA

Published by
Rupa Publications India Pvt. Ltd 2020
7/16, Ansari Road, Daryaganj
New Delhi 110002

Sales Centres:
Allahabad Bengaluru Chennai
Hyderabad Jaipur Kathmandu
Kolkata Mumbai

ISBN: 978-93-90356-04-1

First impression 2020

10 9 8 7 6 5 4 3 2 1

Printed at HT Media Ltd. Gr. Noida

The moral right of the author has been asserted.

Dedicated to
All those who forget to love themselves a little
To all of us

One

—

'Let's get to the packing quickly!' my mom exclaimed.

I was heading to Scotland for my master's degree. Think about it. You dream about something and that dream comes true. That's what I felt when I heard that I would be going to my dream school. Everything was a rush and time was flying by.

'Yes, Maa, I'm going to get to it. There's still some time. Take it easy,' I explained.

'Arre, fine! But just make sure you remember everything you need to pack—be careful about everything,' she said.

'Haan Maa, I'll be careful. I need to visit my friends, spend some time with them and bid them goodbye before I leave,' I said.

'Yes, sure, beta,' my mom agreed.

It's a difficult thing, you know, to leave a house full of memories, full of love and affection. And yet, at the same time, there are things to look forward to, things that are really exciting, things that are intimidating at the same time.

'I'm going to plan a short visit to meet my friends,' I told her.

I invest the most in people. After all, we come alone in this world, earn, spend and live, but if we don't have someone to enjoy the good things in life then what's the point really? So I scrolled through my phone for bus and train tickets for a date on which I could visit my friends.

'Bacha, make a real quick trip to your friends and come back soon,' my dad said.

'I will, I will.'

I could sense the urgency in their eyes and their voices. They wanted to spend more time with me. I packed real quick and booked my ticket to Delhi two days later. And on reaching Delhi, a feeling of immediate happiness flushed my face. This happiness was real, soothing, heart-melting. The kind that makes your already-bright-day brighter.

'Dude, come pick me up,' I called a friend.

'Haan haan, don't you worry, Aveera,' he said and hung up.

Friends, I tell you, are very weird creatures. They make you do things you wouldn't want to do and make you say things you wouldn't want to say. It is almost as if they are your inner voice, except they ring out much louder.

'Yaar, I'm at the station…it's been a while that I've been waiting for you—*aaja ab, hadh hoti hai* (come now, it's too much)' I said, agitated. I was standing at the station, waiting, wearing a flowery dress that draped my thin physique.

'Yes man, I'll reach in two. Real quick,' Kabir said.

Trying to be patient, I happened to see an uncle trying to buy a magazine from a shopkeeper. He seemed to be having a hard time. I reached up to him and asked him what the problem was.

'Beta, actually… I have been trying to buy a newspaper but I do not have change. The shopkeeper is asking me to buy other things to make up for it. But I don't want anything else,' he said, disappointed.

'Arre uncle, that's not an issue. I'll buy the paper for you,' I said, handing a ten rupee note to the shopkeeper.

'No, no, please don't. It's okay, I will buy other things and pay him, it's fine. You don't need to bother yourself,' he replied.

'Uncle, it's just ten rupees. Let me pay. It's completely all right,' I said. I couldn't help but notice a huge smile on the uncle's face. He seemed so elated at that moment and I wanted to keep that moment in my memory forever.

'Thank you. Thank you so much, beta. You're very nice. It's not about a ten rupee note but the values you hold,' he said and blessed me.

The moment felt surreal. You never know the little things that life can offer you, bringing others around you so much joy. I was happier now. My phone suddenly rang. 'Seriously now? Come fast na. I'm outside the station,' Kabir, my friend, said. I immediately ran outside.

'So good to see you, man! It's been a while! I've missed you,' I said, giving him a hug.

'Same here. This city feels better now,' he said, and we drove towards Delhi University North Campus. The drive reminded me of the good old days, and of college. It was a different world back then. Dreamy, full of roses, everything was just painted pink.

'How time flies. We've graduated…you're going to move to Scotland for your master's soon. Everyone has something or the other on their plate. It feels like everything is slipping away,' he said.

'Yeah, I agree. It's hard to watch. But truth be told, it's also kind of good to look forward to things,' I replied with some maturity, clearly feeling low otherwise. This is the beauty, or whatever you want to say about life; it just surprises you in ways you possibly cannot imagine.

'Let's drop in at our college for a bit, na,' I suggested.

I wanted to pay our alma mater a visit. As we reached, the gatekeeper welcomed us with a smile, *'Arre wah ji, aayiae.'* I was surprised to find that he remembered us! I regard him to be one whose friendship that I have earned in the course of my life. As we walked in, we felt great because, hey, we had the best times here. The purest time, I should say.

'Hi ma'am,' I called out to one of my favourite teachers who was just passing by.

'Oh! Bacha, how are you? What are you doing these days?' she asked with excitement.

'I'm good, ma'am. Just preparing for my master's. I'm moving to Scotland for a year or so. How are you? I hope you miss our batch?' I quipped.

'Of course, I do. Your batch was the best,' she responded sincerely.

We started walking towards the canteen area after biding our teacher goodbye. Now, this is important. Our canteen was the best part of the campus. The area defined Hansraj College.

'Chal, let's go to the canteen and have some iced tea,' I grabbed Kabir's hand, pulling him towards the canteen.

'Oh ho, *yeh kaun aaya* (look who's here),' the canteen-waale-bhaiya excitedly exclaimed, and placed his hand on mine to bless me. He was also a friend, more like a father-figure. We shared an amazing bond during my days in college. 'Ice tea?' he asked while I felt nostalgic.

'Haha, yes! You remember!' I said, laughing.

'Of course, you people used to finish all of it,' he said. Kabir and I took the iced tea and sat down, reminiscing the past the entire time. Everything still felt quite fresh; the memories were still alive.

'Yaar, let's eat something as well,' Kabir said, probably

thinking about the famous chowmein at our college canteen.

'Sure, why not! I know what you have in your mind,' I said, smiling wickedly. Kabir laughed with the same wickedness and we ordered some chowmein even though we weren't all that hungry at the time. But who needs to be hungry for chowmein from the canteen? As soon as the food arrived, we felt that we had become the same happy people we used to be. Only now consumed by a more innate happiness. It was just so good.

'Accha, what's next? What do you want to do?' Kabir asked me.

'Let's go to your place, chill there for a bit and then make some plans for the evening?' I suggested.

'Sounds like a plan,' he responded.

Off we went to Kabir's place only to realize that a surprise party had been planned for me. All my friends were present. I felt a moment of sheer joy.

'Oh man! I love you guys!' I exclaimed with happiness in my eyes. It felt like God had bestowed upon me the best of friends in life. Kabir's house had a huge lobby with an open party area. As I walked around the lobby, I saw the entire place decorated with photographs from our college days. There were gifts lying on one corner by the lamp, and sitting on the sofas were my excited friends.

'We love you too, Aveera,' said Poonam, one of my close friends from college. She was known to be the party planner of our group. I knew in my mind that she must have put in much of her time planning this with Kabir.

'Farewell, amigo,' came a voice from behind, which was none other than my overly-dramatic friend, Adi. Adi was our non-serious friend. He found ways to laugh in even the toughest of situations. Sometimes we didn't know if it was the right thing to do but regardless, he was the most-loved in our group.

'Ha ha, yes man. You all are going to be here while I'll have major FOMO out there,' I said.

'C'mon! You are going to Scotland; what's wrong with you?' said Kabir with disappointment.

'Yeah, yeah,' I said, just not wanting to talk about my leaving at this moment.

'Come, I have something for you,' he said and took me up the stairs.

'Here,' he said, handing me a romance novel. 'This book is for you.' It was a thoughtful gift considering I lived in my own dream world.

'Thank you so much. This means a lot,' I replied, after which we both went back to the party to enjoy the rest of the evening.

Downstairs, the door creaked slowly and my other friends were there to surprise me. The best surprise was seeing Rishika there. Rishika was my childhood best friend who stayed in Punjab. She had been my constant since day one! She was one person who knew me the best. I could go to her for any problem.

'Oh my god, Rishika! How come you are here? Don't you have that internship interview tomorrow?' I asked as I hugged her.

'Haha, surprise! Well, Kabir made sure we all came together, and I'll leave early tomorrow so I'll be on time for my interview. So don't worry about that,' she said, giving Kabir a smile.

'Guys, this is so sweet yaa,' I said and hugged them.

I went ahead and met other friends who had come to meet me, and it just felt so magical. Each person you care for counts at the end of the day; the way they make you feel is priceless. We had a few cocktails and the party grew more interesting.

'I'm gonna miss you—a lot,' I pointed at Kabir.

'I know, me too—a lot,' he responded. At which point

my other friends, Poonam and Swati, ambled over, seeking a conversation. Swati was my first friend in college but we had initially drifted apart only to become closer by the end of our college days.

'Aveera, I think it's a wonderful thing that you're getting to go to your dream school. Trust me, there's so much to look forward to in life,' said Poonam.

'Yes, I'm sure. I am looking forward to it,' I replied, a little hesitation and tipsiness lacing my voice. We all danced like there was no tomorrow, and cried a little because the party wouldn't have been complete without a few tears. Even though I was going to be away only for some time, it felt like forever.

The dancing and tears over, around 3.30 a.m., we all sat down on the floor and just started to discuss where we were, and everything else about life…

'You know, who thought we'd be here—sitting like mature adults, talking about life,' Sahil, a dear friend, said. Sahil, the most mature yet so innocent guy of our group. He was always everyone's go-to person in times of crisis. He always talked sense, facts and logic. Sometimes, though, it felt like he was way too direct with his words.

'I know, right?' replied Poonam, in complete agreement.

'I think it's the same—*abb ham bade ho gaye hai*—drama. We're grown up now. We've been prepared for this day anyway,' said Swati, and the others nodded as well.

It was as if everyone had suddenly grown up in a single evening. Here we were, talking as if we had lived through everything.

'Do you think once we grow up, we'll be able to stay in touch and have nights like these?' asked Aseem, another friend from college.

'Yeah, yeah, I'm sure. It's all about the intent,' I responded. But I wasn't sure. *Who knew what the intent will be when we actually cross some stages of our lives?* I thought.

'I think what matters most is that we all stick with one another, especially in times of need. It doesn't matter if we are constantly in touch or not. That's the true essence of friendship,' exclaimed Poonam. Everyone has a notion or two regarding friendship and friends. But the truth is, it's only time that can tell what will last and what won't. *And as they say, go with the flow...*

We were all nostalgic with flashbacks, the memories, even the times to come. Oh, and we sure did enjoy what we had— the present.

The next morning, I met some of my other friends and shopped a bit. Time flew by rather quickly and it was almost time to go back home, to bid adieu to Delhi University and Delhi for a while.

'It's hard yaar, Kabir; you build homes in people and then you get comfortable there and soon, it's time to leave,' I confided.

'But this is what life is. It's not all roses. You've to stop building homes in people and places,' he said while swooshing through the traffic on our way to the railway station.

But, I thought, *who knows if it's too bad a thing to think that there is more or to feel a little more than there's to feel, to see more than there's to see...*

'All right then. It's time. Take care buddy! You've been an amazing friend. There's a lot of good things written in your destiny,' I said to Kabir with tears in my eyes.

He gave me a hug and replied, 'You too, you too. Life is going to be beautiful ahead. Take care.'

I boarded the train, waved Kabir goodbye and left for home.

The journey of a few hours quickly passed, and I traversed thoughts and questions of all kinds.

What is life going to be like? I'm stepping out of my comfort zone and going away from the people I love the most.

And I responded to to my own thoughts, comforting myself. *Arre, it's going to be fine, Aveera, just trust the process.*

But what if all your friends move on with their lives and you are left alone?

All right! Enough! I quashed the negativity, asking my brain to shut up for a while. I wanted to just go with the flow, to cherish the new experiences I was going to have.

The train I was travelling on, a part of the India Railways, served us some good soup and a hearty meal during the rest of the journey and I opened my book. I wanted to focus on reading it.

'I've read that book, it's good,' exclaimed a young man sitting beside me. He had a sharp nose and a wheatish complexion and was dressed in formal clothes. I couldn't help but notice his sleeves rolled up, making him look attractive. 'I think you are travelling abroad soon?' he inquired to my surprise.

'Oh, yes, how did you know?' I asked with a little hesitation evident in my voice.

'Just…you know…instinct,' he replied with a wicked smile.

I didn't reply to his comment. I couldn't stop wondering if I had ever met this man or if I knew him and had forgotten who he was. But nothing really came to mind. I considered and decided that I would not converse with him, despite the fact that there were two hours left in the journey.

But he spoke again, with that wicked smile, 'Don't worry. I just have good instincts, that's all.' He then started to read a newspaper he had by his side.

I couldn't doubt him yet but I was startled. His words made me uncomfortable, and I felt that he gave off a bad vibe. Regardless, I was inquisitive to know more about his 'instinct'.

'You know what, tell me more about yourself,' I asked him, curious as I was.

'Well, I'm a doctor.' He responded as if that finished the conversation, and he got up from his seat and went away. It was weird. I kept looking at him until he closed the door behind him.

He might have gone to the washroom, I thought to myself.

But, even much later, he was nowhere to be seen. The train hadn't even made a stop anywhere. *Where could he have gone? Had he changed his seat?* I kept wondering.

But as I was about to reach my hometown, I ignored thoughts of that young man. He was probably just passing the time with someone else with his strange comments. A while later, I got off the train. My brother was there, smiling, waiting to take me home. 'Yo, aagayi (you're here)? I'm sure you didn't want to come back, huh?' he said.

'Ha ha, nothing like that, Tej bhaiya,' I said, even though what he had said was partially the truth.

'Chal, everyone's waiting for you. You've hardly got five days here before you leave,' he said.

'Yeah, I know,' I said, and thoughts of the journey faded away in that short drive to my home. The door opened as soon we reached. 'My darling daughter,' my mom hugged me as soon as she saw me.

'Mom, I've just been gone for two days, ha ha,' I laughed.

'Yes, but you're going to be gone for a while now. Your first time abroad…' she said with a sad face.

'C'mon, ma,' I said and hugged her back. Everyone at home

tends to be sentimental on a regular basis. I think it just runs in the family.

'Chalo, come in…have something to eat,' she said. I went in to meet my grandma, who was all smiles in her beautiful salwar kameez, waiting to put her hand on my head to bless me. My dad, brother and grandfather were also in the room, busy watching the news on television and just nodded a 'hi' from far away!

'Eat something, for you'll have to cook for yourself for the next year or so now,' my grandmother urged.

'Okay, granny,' I responded and sat down to dinner with them.

The family, all of us, liked to sit together and eat our meals—especially dinner. It was the one thing a family could do together, we felt.

'All right, ma…I'll go to sleep now. I'm a little tired after the journey,' I said as I got up from the table and went off to my room. As I walked towards the door, I began to think about how important families are, how important their lives are in ours. *This is what we live for, right? Love, family and friends. Their happiness, their good health, their everything. If they affect us, if they matter to us…*thinking about all this, I drifted off to sleep.

The next few days were spent shopping and packing. It was a little chaotic. Everyone had something or the other to contribute, and the way of these things is that you have to listen to all their suggestions, whether you agree or not.

'Beta, I need to talk to you,' said my mom, coming into my room the day before I was leaving.

'Tell me,' I replied, keeping aside the notebook I was writing on, about the things I needed to do before leaving for Scotland.

'I just wanted to say this: since you are going away—'

'Arre, Ma, no lecture please…I have been away from home for three years before this as well. It's not a big deal,' I cut her mid-sentence.

'I know you have been, but I am your mother. I am concerned. I'm always going to be concerned,' she said, the worry showing on her face.

'Okay, Ma, tell me, what is it?' I said, finally relenting.

Mom smiled widely, picked up the corner of her dupatta from the ground and pulled out two chairs out in the lawn. She made me sit next to her.

'It's nothing much; I just want to urge you to be careful—careful of everything that will come in your life there. You'll be in a different country. I know there will be things you'll be lured towards. Just know—what lines to cross and what not to,' she said, with a hint of worry on her face. I could see her eyes narrowed with care and concern. At this moment, I realized that I needed to pay more attention to what she was saying to avoid unnecessary stress and worry.

'Right, ma, don't worry. I get it. I'm an adult, I'll know what choices to make,' I replied with confidence. I had a strong will, after all. At this age, one is likely to think they're right every time, that they probably know everything and that there's a generation gap between them and their parents, which, indeed, is true at times.

Anyway, to my answer she said, 'Now, implement this in your life. Don't just nod. And learn to cook—not because you are a girl but because every person on this earth should be self-sufficient. You should know how to feed yourself in times of need.'

'Okay, mommy, anything else?' I said, bored with the turn this conversation had taken.

'Nahin, that's it. Be alert always. I love you,' she said.

'I love you too, mom,' I replied and gave her a peck on the cheek and resumed my packing. I had a flight to catch the next day. My brother was to drop me off at the airport, and a few of my friends were also coming directly to the airport to bade me goodbye.

'All right, my beautiful family. It's time to go,' I said with tears, almost dreading to see the end of the day. I got up from the sofa, after having the last sip of my tea. My grandmother and grandfather got up from their chairs placed right next to me and it all felt like a movie to me. My brother picked up my bags lying next to the dining table and went to keep them in the car. My grandmother hugged me and started to sob. I couldn't control my tears. I hugged her tight, and began to sob too.

'Take care, I love you and will always do so,' she said.

'I love you too, granny,' I said through tears. Turn by turn, I hugged everyone and my heart ached seeing them shed tears. We walked from our lobby towards the main door.

Finally, my brother and I sat in the car and started our journey to the airport. The journey was full of emotions and thoughts, all of which seemed to conquer me.

'*Chill kar* (just chill),' my brother comforted me.

'Ha, yeah,' I said, wiping my tears away. It was hard to say goodbye, but many adventures awaited me.

Two

'**P**lease, *aage chaliye* (proceed),' the uniformed man at the gate said as I showed him my passport to enter the airport. I turned around and smiled at my brother, waving goodbye. As my eyes met Kabir's, a small teardrop escaped. There's something about airports and railway stations; there are so many people with packed bags. Some of them are arriving, while some are leaving—God knows where for. You don't know anyone at these places, but you relate to them. Like a passenger in this life who sometimes has an idea regarding where he's headed, and at other times, no idea at all...

'I love you guys,' I whispered as I looked through the glass window, moving towards my check-in counter. I completed all the formalities and waited near my designated gate.

Near the boarding gate, an aunty sitting beside me asked, 'You'll have a parantha, beta?'

'No, aunty, thank you,' I said and smiled.

She looked like she was a Punjabi as well, and I immediately thought about my mother, who had insisted that I take a parantha for the journey. I guess all mothers are alike here—it is a very Punjabi, rather, an Indian thing to do.

'Beta, you are also going to Canada?' she asked.

'Ha, no aunty! This is the boarding gate for Scotland,' I replied.

'Oh, really?' she exclaimed, immediately checking her boarding pass to realize that she was sitting near the wrong gate.

'Thank you, beta ji,' she said hurriedly and left for her boarding gate. 'No problem,' I said as I saw her leave.

She must be visiting her family in Canada. What a relief that she hadn't missed her flight. She would be reunited with her kids and family who had probably shifted there, I imagined.

'Boarding for Scotland now. Business class passengers please come to Gate Two,' the speakers boomed. I sat there patiently, waiting for the other passengers to board. I always board at the end; I mean, what's the point of standing in a queue for no reason? I sat there, observing the people rushing here and there. One can only learn through observation. Finally, I was the last to board...or so I thought.

'Mr Aryan! Final announcement for Mr Aryan,' I heard and saw a young man walking in—a face so familiar that I had to shake my head a little to check if I was dreaming! It was none other than the guy on the train, who had told me he was a doctor, boarding the same flight as me. What were the odds? *Anyway, I now know his name,* I thought. He didn't look at me or maybe pretended not seeing me. Or maybe I was overthinking it...

I did what a normal millennial would do—I stalked him! I know we were supposed to switch off our phones but I couldn't contain my curiosity and opened Facebook and Instagram both. But unfortunately, with limited signal and a lot of Aryans, I couldn't find him. I had hoped we would have some mutual friends or a connection of some kind, but the airplane had to fly, and I had to switch my phone off. I prayed to God as the plane readied for take-off.

The journey was smooth and quiet until I was interrupted

from watching a movie by someone who had suddenly come by.

'Hi,' I said, looking at that strange young man—oh sorry, Aryan. He was casually dressed and seemed a little different, wearing sneakers and pyjamas with a shaved face. Oddly enough, I remembered him in smartly dressed formals.

'Now I didn't know you were going to Scotland,' he said and smiled.

'Oh, haha, yeah,' I said, taking little interest in talking to him.

'Come to the back—aren't you tired of sitting here? There is five more hours to go,' he invited me.

'Oh, yeah. Sure,' I replied, even though I didn't want to go. I don't know what made me get up and follow him to his seat at the back. From the start I had been determined to not talk to this weird person at all. I questioned myself—*What is this sudden magnetic pull that you have to talk to him?*

'So, how've you been?' he asked.

'I'm good, thanks. You tell me. How have you been?' I asked, still questioning myself for asking him such an open question even though I had little to no interest in him.

'Great!' his response was a single word.

We stood in silence for a few minutes. And then, he looked towards me, gave me that same wicked smile I remembered and looked out of the plane through a window. I blushed a little, not knowing what made him smile. But without saying another word, he left.

I called out to him as he turned away, 'Aryan!'

A few passengers turned to look at me. I guess I had spoken a bit too loudly.

When Aryan turned around, he seemed surprised. 'Yeah?' he asked, nonchalant and carefree.

A little embarrassed, I said, 'Oh, actually it's nothing. Forget it,' and returned to my seat. I put on my headphones and resumed watching my movie, even though I knew I couldn't focus on the scene or the characters.

Why is he behaving in such a manner? And moreover, why am I responding to everything he's saying? Why do I feel such a magnetic pull? I kept thinking about it for a while. I couldn't really silence my mind. At the beginning of the flight all I had wanted to do was watch the movie and not focus on anything else. *Look how that turned out.*

'Chill,' I heard a voice from behind me. The music in my headphones wasn't loud enough. It was Aryan again. He was trying to mess with me.

'Yeah, sure. I'm chill. Don't you worry,' I responded curtly.

The following four hours passed quietly; we didn't talk at all. I kept my calm for the rest of the flight and avoided any contact with Aryan even though I couldn't stop thinking about him and his odd behaviour. I didn't know when I had fallen asleep, only to wake up to the announcement, 'Welcome to Glasgow Airport.' I rubbed my eyes and opened them to finally realize that we had reached Scotland. I prayed and thanked God for the safe flight and then it was time to get off. I completed the formalities at the airport and stood at the baggage claim, waiting for my bag. Usually at airports, my bag is late to arrive but luckily this time, it was one of the first. I collected my baggage, booked an Uber to the school and as I was about to leave, I remembered and turned back to see if Aryan was anywhere to be seen. But I couldn't find him anywhere. *He's probably already left or something,* I thought to myself and left.

Three

Having located my Uber, we started off. I looked around Glasgow through the window; it was such a beautiful place to be. There was a chill in the air, but it felt like the kind of cold that makes you warm inside. Or maybe, I had just arrived and was being naïve; the reality was still to set in. I texted my family's WhatsApp group, telling them that I had landed and that I was in an Uber. Safe and sound.

'That's great!'

'Oh, thank God.'

'May God bless you,' were the replies that I received from my family. *It's funny how our parents have become more active on social media these days than any of us. They seem to enjoy it more and are probably more hooked than us,* I surmised distractedly.

'I'll call once I reach the hostel,' I replied. I also texted Kabir. I wanted to talk to him.

I smiled and put my phone away. The drive was so beautiful I did not want to miss a single glimpse of it. I was in awe. It made me fall in love with nature all over again. It had been a while since I had last seen such greenery.

I was almost at the school when I realized this was all real. I was on my own in a beautiful country and would be here for one year. It was nice, you know, to be there, or at least I felt that way at the moment. I reached the school gates, got off the Uber and thanked the driver. The school was nothing less than what I had dreamed of. There were big gates already open for the students. The entire place was buzzing with students as almost everyone had just arrived. There were registration and help desks right near the main gate of the school.

'Hi, could you please help me with the location of the R halls?' I asked the lady sitting at the help desk. She looked like a senior year student to me who was volunteering.

'Sure, here you go,' she handed me the map. 'Just keep walking straight and to your right, you'll find the R halls,' she said with a huge smile on her face. After that she noted down my school ID and completed certain formalities to register me in the system.

'Thanks, cheers,' I said and went ahead. Some people near the gate were kind enough to help me with my luggage. I looked at the map the lady gave me to understand a bit more about the route. The school was full of greenery and it seemed like a natural park in there.

The walk to my hostel was adorned with plants and trees on both sides. There was a lawn in front of the hostel as well, with cute benches around it. It suddenly began to pour; I heard the patter of rain drops. It seemed as if the sky was welcoming me to Scotland, its arms open wide. I quickly walked into the hostel and filled all the forms at the reception. They handed me the keys to my room with a smile.

I didn't know who to expect as my roommate but I was quite excited about that.

As I entered the lift lobby, a sudden flutter of butterflies churned my stomach. I was just anxious to get to experience this new chapter of my life. I didn't know who I would have to live with but I was quite excited.

My flat was a mixed flat with five rooms in total. I passed through the kitchen, which seemed well equipped, then the washrooms, the common area and finally, I saw my room. Room number 6B. Excitement coursed through me at the thought of a new home all to myself. I opened the door and saw an exceptionally maintained room. There was a cupboard right next to the door and a whiteboard above my bed to place any pictures or mementos. A beautiful study table with a table lamp was right next to my bed. It wasn't a very big room but big enough for me! I opened the curtains to witness a beautiful scene outside. I could see beautiful trees swaying as the raindrops touched them. It smelled and felt good. I was happy in that very moment. I dropped my stuff on the floor and called my mother.

'The room is pretty great, Ma, I just reached,' I said.

'Yeah? Facetime with me, I'll also take a look,' she said. My mother is very fond of Facetiming. I called her on Facetime and showed her the room, moving my phone in angles to show her the sight outside the window.

'Wow, Aveera. It's such a nice room,' she finally said.

'Right? I love it,' I replied.

'But make sure you keep it that way! You're bad at maintaining and taking care of things,' she exclaimed.

'Oh god, mom, not again. I know. I will take care of things. You don't worry about it,' I replied, exasperated.

'Also, make sure you're eating on time, and eat properly. Oh ruko, let me finish…' her voice grew softer as my dad took over.

'Beta, have you checked who your flatmates are and are you feeling okay there?' he asked.

'Yes, dad. I'm feeling okay. But I'm not yet sure who my flatmates are going to be,' I told him.

'Okay, be aware of everything. You are on your own now.

Take decisions for yourself—like a smart and mature adult. And focus on your studies properly,' he said.

I chuckled. *Dads and moms are so different and so are their priorities,* I thought. *Together they manage to create a balance in our lives.*

'Okay, Dad. I will be careful about everything. I'll go unpack my things and relax a little. I love you guys,' I said.

'Love you, beta, bye,' they chorused as I hung up. I had one more call to make.

I called Kabir. 'Hey babe, I just reached my hostel,' I said.

'Hey, how are you feeling?' he asked.

'Yeah, I am feeling good. The place is quite nice. It's raining right now. I guess this is how it's going to be most of the time. I miss you,' I said finally, happy to hear his voice.

'C'mon, you've just been gone for a day! You'll be fine. I miss you too,' he reassured me.

'Yeah, all right. I'll get some rest and unpack.'

'Okay, bye. Take care. Love you,' Kabir said.

'Love you,' I said as I hung up. I took a deep breath and looked outside the window. *I guess this is my home then!* I told myself.

I unpacked a few things but was too tired to arrange them. I kept the stuff I would immediately need and decided I would unpack later. I had the rest of the day and the night to get things in order. Moreover I was inquisitive, so I went out to check out my flat and saw a girl standing in the kitchen. I went in.

'Oh, hi!' she said, looking at me.

'Hi, I'm Aveera. I've been allotted a room here,' I said.

'Hi Aveera, I'm Ally, I'm in Room 6A.'

'Nice to meet you, Ally. Where are you from?'

'I'm from the States, how about yourself?' she asked, picking up a cup of coffee and asking me if I wanted one as well with a gesture.

'Sure,' I responded. I wanted some coffee. 'Well, I'm from India,' I said as I took the filled cup from her hands.

'Oh, that's amazing. I love India. I've been there once. I visited the Taj Mahal,' she said with a pronounced American accent.

'Oh, really? That's amazing. I'm glad you liked it. We'll plan your visit there again sometime soon. It's a huge country with a lot to explore,' I said, pride filling me, and I kept boasting a little about India. It's funny how we keep cribbing about our country while we are there, but the moment we step out of the country, the feeling of pride kicks in and we become—as they call them—deshbhakts.

'Yes, yes, sure. So which course are you taking?' she asked me.

'I'm going to be studying Strategic Management. What about you?'

'I'm in Management too but I'm in the Financial Management course,' she answered.

'Oh! Finance! Nice. I'm always in awe of people in finance. You guys have a lot to work on, I bet it requires a lot of studying.'

'Ha, I guess it's all about what you're interested in. I enjoy finance,' she said with a smile.

'Yeah, totally. I get what you're saying,' I returned the smile; it felt like I had made a friend already. *Nice!*

'Anyway, I'll see you soon. I just need to run some errands,' she said, putting down her cup. 'I've been here for two days. Take my number since we'll be needing each other quite often.'

'Yes, give it to me,' I said, handing my phone to her to save her number.

'Great! I'll see you around,' she said and left.

'See you.'

I took my still unfinished cup of coffee with me and went to take a look at the other areas of the flat. There was a television in the common room, a foosball table and some other board games. I walked out of the door to take a look at the rest of the hostel. I preferred to take the vintage staircase, all the while observing everything around me.

Reaching downstairs, I sat down in the main lobby. I could see some brochures and other hostel residents hovering around. Everyone carried their own stories with them. Everyone seemed to have come with some baggage, or some inertia, to get rid of—or so I thought. I must have been looking like a lost bird, observing people and the area around me, so I was not surprised when I heard one of the receptionists walk up to me.

'You all right?' she asked.

'Oh yeah, everything's okay. I've just moved in today so I'm checking out the area…and just observing. Can you guide me to the nearest grocery store?' I asked her.

'Yeah sure, there's Morrisons right at the corner. Just step out of the school, take a right and you'll see Morrisons. It has everything you need. All the pubs and bars are also nearby. They're just a ten-minute walk from the school,' she said, smiling.

'Oh, great! Thanks, that was helpful,' I got up and decided to go back to my room before I got in her way; the reception was rather busy. But it was kind of sweet of her to check on me like that. *Otherwise no one really gives a damn about these little things,* I thought.

I picked up my coffee and put it in the kitchen sink in the common area and then, instead of the stairs, took a lift to go back to my room. I thought my room had the best view.

It was more than I could have asked for. Tired, I thought of taking a quick nap.

It was only after I noticed the lack of any light in the room that I realized I had been sleeping for hours. I woke up feeling a little refreshed, but still jet-lagged, and unpacked the rest of my things. Suddenly, a ping, and then another: messages on the WhatsApp group for Indian students. It had been formed by one of the students and I had joined it a while ago. It would help us get to know each other and get comfortable in a foreign land.

'Let's go to the jazz club at 9.30?' one of the texts by a person named Arun had received some attention. 'Yes', 'Sure', and 'Okay' were the kind of replies I read. I could go as well. 'Okay, sounds good,' I sent a text.

Why not, I thought. I might as well make some friends. It would be nice to know some people, to start this journey with friends around.

The jazz club was lit with beautiful lights and full of really interesting-looking people. I observed all the happy people sitting at the round tables in the club. A lady and her kid were lounging about; some larger groups of friends were sharing smiles.

'Hi, you're Aveera, right?' a voice spoke behind me.

'Hi, yes,' I said as I turned around, only to find Aryan standing there.

'What? You?'

'Yeah, me. I'm doing a PhD in Medicine here,' he responded.

'Oh!' was the only response I could muster. His eyes were gleaming, his skin glowing and he looked absolutely handsome which I had never noticed in all our weird encounters earlier. His sharp nose and thin fingers holding on to a glass were a treat to my eyes.

'Nice to see you,' he said.

I shook my head a bit to come back to my senses and responded quickly, 'Yeah, sure.' I still did not want any further conversation with him. I couldn't understand what had been happening all this while. *Maybe he looked into my profile through some school website or link*, I thought. But it still made me very apprehensive.

'Listen, relax. I've just been messing with you. I found you on the group for international students and happened to see you on the train. And it was a coincidence that we were on the same flight. Please chill,' he said.

I wanted to believe what he just said. After all, it made sense. But I still felt that magnetic pull towards him and it made very anxious.

'Okay, fine. I mean how else would you know me? But why do you have to be so weird about all this?' I questioned him.

'Haha, it's just who I am. Anyway, *sabhi kuch abhi poochna hai kya?*' He asked if I wanted to ask everything right away, then he shook his head and went to socialize with other people.

'Well yeah, all right,' I said, leaving to meet the others myself.

I introduced myself with a quick smile and repeated my name, sometimes four or five times, as I move around the room. Everyone was new. They seemed like a fun bunch to talk to and hang out with.

'Hey, nice to meet you. Where are you from?' asked a girl, introducing herself as Ruchi. She was tall, with a wheatish complexion and extremely long hair.

'Nice to meet you too, Ruchi. I'm from Ambala. How about you?' I asked.

'I'm from Delhi,' she responded.

'Oh, really? I studied and lived there for three whole years.

I love Delhi. My entire friend circle is in Delhi,' I said with a lot of excitement and enthusiasm. I felt like I'd be able to connect with this girl since she must have been raised in Delhi; she would understand my responses and the nuances of my character, most of which I'd picked up in college.

'That's amazing, where did you go? I went to LSR. Did my English honours there,' she responded.

'Oh, I went to Hansraj. For Commerce.' I told her.

'Oh, Hansraj! That's nice…I really think the people who went to North Campus had a much better graduation experience than the others,' she said with a genuine smile, continuing to talk about Hansraj and the campus. Delhi University has two campuses. One is the North Campus and the other is South Campus. Most of the best colleges are located in the North Campus, so, it's lively and engaging in terms of activities around the area. People prefer the campus more than they prefer actually looking for a particular college. There's a lot to do around there, a lot of food joints and a lot of places to chill.

'Haha, I'll happily agree to that. Campus was a lot of fun. So, which course are you pursuing here?' I asked her.

'I'll be doing FM,' she responded. Another Finance student.

'Oh, my flatmate here is also going to pursue the same course. I can introduce you to her,' I responded.

'Oh yeah? That'll be great. What's her name?'

'Ally. She's from the States. Seems like a nice girl.'

'Okay. Cool. I'll talk to her when I get the chance.'

'Perfect, let's get a drink?' I asked.

We both went to the bar area where everyone else had gathered. I conversed with people over some beer, but only a few. I had decided that I would take it easy since I was sleepy and with new people.

'Yo! Enjoying yourself?' asked none other than Aryan, who seemed to be around wherever I was.

'Yeah, you tell me? How's it going for you?' I asked him, returning his comment with a wicked smile, the kind that he normally had on his face. *Why not act with him the same way he has been behaving with me?* I thought.

'Oh, I see what you did there,' he replied, laughing.

'Oh, accha, you did?' I said in a sarcastic tone. He was annoying me. His magnetic eyes were gripping but he still annoyed me a lot.

'Haha, I'm enjoying myself, madam. This place seems fun,' he responded, all the while seeming to be preoccupied.

'Yeah, indeed. I have heard a lot about Scotland and Europe. It's quite beautiful,' I replied with a smile on my face, trying to ease into the conversation.

Suddenly he reached out and touched my forehead. I felt numb and couldn't react. 'You had something on your forehead,' he explained, removing it.

'Oh,' I said. I could feel my heart beating fast, but at the same time, I felt a little uncomfortable. 'Okay, no problem. I could have removed it myself,' I said, making a face.

'Dude, chill. I hope you're not thinking I'm interested in you or something.' he suddenly said.

'Yeah, whatever,' I said, feeling a little embarrassed, at which point he made a weird face and went around to talk to the others.

The evening passed uneventfully after that. There was much discussion about the past and what Scotland was going to look like for us new inhabitants. It was a fun evening of getting to know people and laughing with others. Finally, some of us called it a night, shared phone numbers and left for the hostel.

I walked back with Ruchi while talking more about our

lives in Delhi and the expectations we had from Scotland.

'Chal, bro. I'm on the fourth floor,' said Ruchi, giving me a quick hug and left.

'Okay bro, bye. I'll see you around.'

Reaching my room, I was quite tired and it didn't take me much time to crash into my bed and fall asleep.

Four

Next morning, I woke up with a smile. I was beginning to like the vibe of this place.

I had a free day to explore the city so I got up, Facetimed my parents and also called Kabir. Kabir, let me tell you about Kabir.

Kabir is my best friend, my go-to person. He is the one person who will just drop everything else to come be with me. He has the most gorgeous smile and the most amazing hair. His charming personality and his warm aura attract so many around him. Oh, and his intelligence is never to be doubted. I think I probably developed feelings for him at some point. I loved him—for all I knew or cared to know. I still love him with all my heart.

'Hey, Kabir. How are you?' I asked.

'All well. You tell me? How is Scotland? How are you adjusting to the place?' he asked.

'Well, umm…yeah, it's good. I went out yesterday. Met some people from India. Socialized,' I replied.

'Oh, that sounds fun. Enjoy yourself.'

'Yeah,' I replied and kept quiet.

'What's up? Why so low?' he questioned.

'Nothing. Not low actually,' I replied. 'Chal, I think I'm going to go and explore, see what the city has to offer,' I said with a smile.

'All right, bye. Take care. See you soon,' he said and hung up.

I quickly showered and remembered that I had to go shop for groceries and some basic things. I took out my phone and texted Ruchi.

'Hey, you free to hang out today? Need to shop for some basic things,' I wrote.

And immediately Ruchi replied. 'Aveera! Yes, I am. I too had to shop for some groceries. See you downstairs in ten minutes?'

I responded quickly, telling her I would see her soon. As I stepped out of my room, I saw two guys standing in the kitchen along with Ally, chatting. I went in to say hello.

'Oh, hi! You must be our fourth flatmate?' said an exceptionally good-looking guy.

'Hi, yes, I'm Aveera,' I responded with a smile.

'I'm Andrew and he's Lance, my boyfriend,' he said, a cute blush spreading across his face.

'Hi, Lance. Nice to meet you both. So, where are you guys from?' I asked, my interest piqued. I've always wanted to get to know people who are openly gay, chat with them. I have always thought that they are more open and more accepting in the way they perceive their lives. Their minds are broader, and somehow, they are more warm.

'Well, I'm from Paris and Andrew is from Spain,' Lance said, holding on to Andrew's hand. 'And you? Let me guess—India?' Andrew piped in.

'Yes, I'm from India. How could you've guess?' I asked, surprised.

'He's kidding, he couldn't have guessed. Ally just told us,' Lance spoke and they exchanged a warm look.

'Haha, all right,' I said. 'Anyway, I have to go to the supermarket to get some groceries. But I'll see you guys later?

Maybe we can have dinner together; I can cook something Indian?'

'Yeah! That sounds so good!' responded Ally. Andrew and Lance nodded in agreement.

'Great! I'll see you guys around then!' I responded and left in a rush. I didn't want to keep Ruchi waiting. Ruchi and I shopped for a while, chatting as we drifted along the aisles. We then decided to have lunch and went to a Thai restaurant. Thai food always excited me because of their mild spices and their curries. We ordered Thai green curry with some sticky rice. We talked about our college life and enjoyed the scrumptious food. The décor and ambience of the place added to the delight. The entire place had a vintage feel to it with vintage cutlery and furniture. We went around to shop some more post our lunch. It had turned out to be a rather fun day. As I returned, I felt that I had found a good friend in Ruchi.

Stepping indoors, I saw Aryan again. He looked away while walking past me and went outside. His nonchalance felt odd. I felt bad even though there was no reason for me to feel that way. It was almost as if I had wanted him to notice me and talk to me. Or I wanted to clear the air, speak to him. Surprising myself again, I shouted out, 'Hey, Aryan!'

He turned around, waved and gestured that he was in a hurry and left the hostel.

The odd feeling stayed. The whole affair, slight as it was, affected me way too much. His dismissal hurt my ego and I decided never to speak with him again. I didn't want to continue to feel this way. I had to focus on better things in life.

I stood a while in the kitchen, then began to prepare the dinner I had in mind. I was tired, but I wanted to eat dinner with my flatmates.

All of us decided to prepare one dish each, of our own choice. I made butter chicken with bread. Andrew and Lance made some Spanish omelette filled with veggies. Ally on the other hand brought food from the superstore.

'I was too tired to cook, guys,' she confessed. 'But here, I got us some wine,' she said and opened the wine. Well, clearly everyone was happy.

We put on some nice music, enjoyed and relished the meals, cracked some jokes. That evening ended up becoming quite a good evening. I had such a multicultural experience with my flatmates. Andrew and Lance were the cutest couple I'd ever met. They showered each other with so much love and affection, and most importantly, such freedom.

Later, Ally and I went for a walk and chatted about the food a bit, but it was only when she mentioned the crimes in America that I realized foreign countries are not all that they're made out to be—peaceful and tolerant. It's just that things are highlighted in Indian media more than we realize.

'You know, my best friend, back in the States, faced so much racism. Was almost raped. But there was nothing she could do back then. The country is so vast…hardly any cause gets the attention it deserves,' Ally said.

'Oh damn, I thought only India had such issues,' I said in a rather exhausted tone.

'Coming from a country like the US,' Ally spoke again, 'where we have a lot of notions of it being a progressive country, which I'm sure it is, there's so much that still goes unnoticed. There are people doing dark things everywhere…I have read about so many cases in India too, you know? So many rape cases, so many crimes, it's ghastly!' she said in disappointment.

'I know it is. I feel that Western countries are still more

developed when it comes to the safety of their citizens at least,' I replied.

'Yeah, I guess. But, you know, each person—everywhere in the world—is going through one problem or the other. Everyone has some story to tell. It's hard to interpret who's actually happy,' she pondered out loud. That was the truth, I felt, and it hit me hard. Everyone is fighting some battle. It's just the way life is…' she continued as I waited for her to finish. 'I wanted to make sure to have a one-of-a-kind experience, to learn as much as I could from the people around me, and maybe, become a knowledgeable and broad-minded person. At the end of the day, you learn from each person you meet in your life. Each person has something or the other to teach you.'

'True,' I said warmly. 'Let's see where our life takes us.'

We headed back to the hostel after that, and quietly went to our rooms. The air seemed to have stilled after the heartfelt conversation we had just had.

Later at night, as I was lying down on my bed, I reflected on the conversation I had with Ally. What she had said resonated with me. To make the most of my time here, to learn from everyone I met. This was one of the aims I would have while I was here—to take in as much as I could in the one year that I have.

My classes were to start the next day so I lay down to sleep. I wanted to be fresh the next morning. I was looking forward to enjoying my time here, interacting with the people and making the most of studying in a school abroad.

The morning was bright and the first class of the day went fairly well. The class consisted of introductions, and everyone spoke a few words about themselves. What really made me happy was that the class was quite multicultural. There were so many people and so much to learn from everyone.

'I'm Aveera, from India. I'm hoping to get a vast experience here. I love writing and socializing. So I hope to learn new things from this place,' I said as a matter of introduction. After the day ended, I received a text from Ruchi asking if I wanted to meet and share an evening snack—and maybe a beer, later. I liked the idea.

We went to a bar nearby and had some snacks and a fun time, and yes, discussions too. Ally joined in later. Ally and Ruchi seemed to get along well and I was quite pleased by the development. The three of us hung out, and over a few beers, had lots and lots of conversations.

'I'm definitely enjoying my time here,' Ruchi said.

'Me too. This is my first time in the UK. I have travelled a bit in my life but never really thought I'd end up in Scotland one day to study,' said Ally.

'Yeah, I like this place too. I mean I always thought I'd come here—which eventually happened,' I said.

Ally stopped as she saw a man approaching us, and gestured by way of introduction. 'Oh, by the way, meet my boyfriend, Justin,' she said.

'Hi Justin,' Ruchi and I greeted him in unison.

'Nice to meet you,' he responded gaily.

'So, Justin and I actually met on the flight here. It was love at first sight. He's from England. It might sound weird, but yeah…that's how it happened,' Ally explained, a little shy.

'Wow! Not weird at all…I mean it's great,' I said, surprised and happy for her at the same time. We all sat down for a few more beers until we all were a little tipsy, which signalled the end of the night. We had to go back to our rooms.

On the way back, we talked about the strangest and weirdest

of things. While we were walking from the lawn towards our dorm I saw Aryan, standing and reading a book in the corner like god's gift to humanity.

'Hey, you guys, go on ahead, I'll join you later. Oh, and Ally, tell Andrew and Lance that I won't be able to make it to the club tonight. I'll join them on the weekend. I just have something urgent I have to do right now,' I said tipsily, walking ahead of my friends.

'You sure you'll be all right?' asked Ruchi.

'Yes, yes, go ahead. I'll be fine,' I said, assuring them.

I'd not done this in my wildest dreams, but I walked up to Aryan. 'Hey there, handsome.' I said out loud, blushing. I was red from the beers and from such an open confession.

'Oh, wow…umm. Hi?' Aryan said, looking up from his book.

'That's it? That's all you're going to say?' I asked.

'Are you drunk? Why are you alone? How did you get here?' He scanned the area, looking behind me.

'Mister. Stop with all these questions. I asked you how you were doing,' I tipsily continued.

'I'm good, Aveera. Come, let's go inside. I'll drop you to your room. It's getting late. You should go to sleep, you have classes tomorrow at nine,' he replied.

'How do you even know my timetable?' I questioned, my eyes rolling.

'Now is not the time, Aveera, let's go,' he held my hand and starting walking me to my room.

'You're very handsome, you know that?' I said, knowing fully well that my sober self would never have. I was going to regret doing whatever I was doing and for saying whatever I was saying to Aryan. Regardless, I couldn't stop. I had a crush on him—ever since I'd seen him—him and his weird way of talking and behaving.

He looked me in the eye and said, 'I think you're very beautiful too, Aveera. I really do. But now, we must go inside and you should take some rest.'

'Okay,' I conceded. I couldn't stop blushing, for he had finally said something really sweet. It felt like I had known him for a long, long time. He was giving me the chills, the kind that were unexpected and expected at the same time; the kind that could make your heart go crazy.

'All right, tell me your room number,' he said, holding the lift for us to get in.

'It's 6B,' I said, tightening my grip on his hand.

'Okay, let's go,' he said and pressed the elevator button. I leaned my head on his shoulder as we went up to the sixth floor. We got off the elevator and Aryan led me towards my room.

'Aveera, you all right?' I heard Andrew call out.

'Yes, I'm all right, go, go,' I whispered, not willing to ruin my time with Aryan.

'Chalo,' Aryan said as we entered my flat and he helped me lie down on the bed. He put a comforter on me and brushed my hair with his hand. 'Goodnight, sleep tight,' he said.

'Night,' I replied as I saw him leaving with my hazy eyes. He closed the door behind him and the rest was history. I quickly passed out.

I woke up in the morning with a slight headache which only increased when I realized what I had done last night.

'Oh God! Oh God!' I spoke out loud. 'What the hell!

What did I do, man! Damn! Shit! I cursed myself, finally collecting myself to get up and take a shower. I wondered how I would face Aryan. *I'll just never see him and never talk to him again*, I thought. My embarrassment stuck in my head and I could think of nothing else the whole day.

I wanted to meet him and on the other hand, I just didn't want to ever meet him or even bump into him again. But little did I know that God was probably listening in and I actually didn't see him the whole day.

Not only the whole day, a week passed and he was nowhere to be seen.

I didn't have his number, and he wasn't even on the WhatsApp group for international students. I couldn't even text him and talk about the whole incident with him. It was driving me crazy.

'I don't know what to do,' I confided in Andrew while we were having lunch at our favourite cafe.

'I think you should just keep an eye out for him, and if it's meant to be, you'll probably bump into him soon,' he assured, comforting me.

'Yeah, I really hope I do. Do you think he totally judged me for being so drunk the other day? Maybe he doesn't like people who can't even handle themselves when it comes to alcohol? Maybe he just doesn't like me!' I said, putting my face between my hands.

'Woah, woah woman! Stop! Stop thinking too much. You've got to make me meet this guy when you finally get to see him. I don't know what's *so* good about him. I thought only Lance had the ability to cause this kind of earthquake. But it looks like there's another guy out there who's making people go crazy.'

'All right, I will, and listen—he's not yours,' I said, suddenly possessive about the not-yet-my-boyfriend.

'Haha, yes Ma'am. Now stop going nuts. You'll find him.

He must be busy. He's doing a PhD. Not a master's like the rest of us! Come on,' he said, patting my hand.

'Well, I hope that is the case,' I said, raising my left hand and actually crossing my fingers, suddenly superstitious.

We had our meal in peace after that. Andrew had this quality about him; he calmed people down. Lance, on the other hand, was often hyperactive. They both just somehow balanced each other, in multiple ways. They seemed so perfect together—at least to me.

We left the café to go ahead with the rest of our classes that day. A long day was ahead of us, made even longer because my thoughts were overpowering me, causing me to think about Aryan again and again. I just couldn't make sense about why he had disappeared so suddenly, why he had never tried to make any contact. I tried to bury myself in my studies and forget about it entirely, keeping alive the hope that I would soon see him.

'Everything okay?' Ruchi asked a few days later, while we were having dinner in the flat.

'Yeah…I guess. Actually, I think I like this guy…but I haven't been able to get in touch with him for over a week and it's getting quite annoying,' I said with a frustrated look.

'Oh! Who is this guy?' she asked, interested.

'I'll make you meet him when the time comes. For now, I just want to see where it goes. I'm not even dating him… yet. Maybe the feelings are just one-sided,' I said with a sigh.

'Hmm, all right. Take it easy though. You'll be fine. Anyway, listen. I was thinking, maybe we should plan a trip somewhere— sometime this winter?' she asked, changing the topic.

'Sounds like a good idea,' I told her, happy to have something to look forward to. 'I want to travel now that we're here. It's feasible and should be fun.' I was excited. I finally had something else to think about.

'Great! You talk to your friends. Ally should be up for it, and I think your friends, Andrew and Lance, will be fun to go out with too, no?' she asked.

'Oh yes, they're amazing. They're way too much fun if I'm being honest,' I responded.

'Cool. I'll look up the tickets and see how it goes. We can go to Ireland, or even Paris,' she said, excited.

'I'll check with them and let you know.'

The next few days passed in a blur. We spent it planning the trip and it felt like something good had come to pass in my life. We found tickets for an affordable rate and we decided to go ahead and book them. We were actually going to Paris in a month! It seemed like a dream.

Meanwhile, I had a paper to submit and I got busy, spending hours working in the library. Suddenly, my eyes fell on Aryan! He was sitting in a corner with a book and a pen in his hand. I couldn't help but gaze with longing; my heart nearly sped out of my chest and I felt as if I would burst. A strange feeling came over me, right in my stomach, a feeling I had never felt before. I liked him too much. His touch still felt fresh on my hands, and god knows how badly I wanted another chance to touch him. Almost two weeks had passed since I had last seen him. Without thinking for another second, I got up from my seat and walked towards him.

'Hi,' I greeted chirpily.

'Oh. Hi Aveera,' he said looking up from his book, with such calmness that I almost wanted to sit down right there and kiss him.

'How are you? Where have you been?' I asked, trying my

best to not appear too needy, even as I wanted to shoot millions of questions at him.

'I'm good, actually. I had a lot of submissions so I have been busy. How have you been?' he asked.

'I'm good,' I said quickly, even though what I wanted to say was—I haven't been that great actually! You were lost somewhere and I had no idea how to contact you, or even how to reach out to you. So, it's actually been pretty annoying lately. But I wanted to appear calm and composed. 'Umm…do you want to grab a cup of coffee?' I asked him suddenly, my eyes half closed in anticipation.

'That'd be really nice right now,' he replied. Oh my god! I could imagine the look I must have had on my face. I was happy, so much so that I guess I was blushing.

We both left the library and started to walk towards the café when I felt his hands on mine—he entangled his fingers in mine, criss-crossing and holding on to them like they held a lot of comfort. I returned the grip. I don't know what it was about that moment, but I immediately felt safe, composed, at peace and simply, content.

'Why did you just disappear?' I asked again, softly, hoping for an honest reply.

'I didn't. I was actually in the library all the time, studying for my submissions. A PhD is harder than you think,' he said.

'I'm sure it is,' I replied.

'What's happening with you? I hope you didn't get drunk again?' he asked with a smile.

'Ah, no. I've been busy working on a paper. Also, I'm planning to visit Paris in a month. Just getting the tickets and everything.'

'What, really? That's crazy—I'm travelling to Prague and Paris in a month as well. Maybe we can catch up while we're both there.'

'Oh, woah. Sure thing. I'd love it,' I said. I immediately regretted saying the word 'love' but now that it was said and done, I couldn't really take it back. Instead I made it worse and continued to speak. 'I mean I would like it... I mean I'd love it too, but you know, like it like...actually...yeah whatever,' I stammered and ate some of the words.

'Hahaha,' he laughed, pausing for a moment. 'I'd love it too, Aveera.' He smiled.

At the café, we drank our coffee and enjoyed the rest of the time and went back to the library to work on our respective papers.

On the way back, out of the blue, he suddenly spoke, 'Listen, I like you too, Aveera. I really do, and I might have acted like a weird person, but don't worry, I'm going to stick with you.'

I held tightly on to his hand, feeling the warmth that I had been longing for. All the while I had only been *telling* everyone that I had a connection with him.

'Me too,' I said with a genuine smile.

'Now, go! Work on your paper. It's important you work on it well, and then we'll go for a walk in the evening,' he said very calmly.

Excited, I said, 'Yeah, I'll see you soon.' Then I left to work on my paper.

The whole episode just felt surreal, like something out of a fairy tale. The way things were working for me, it was a dream come true. I felt as if he understood me, without my even having to say a word.

From the corner of my eye, I saw him sitting across the table, engrossed in his work. I gave myself a smile and dug into my work.

Five

The days passed like magic. Life was good, and Aryan was always around, being extremely loving and staying by my side.

Soon enough, I called my mother, 'Hey Ma, I have met someone here. I'll tell you all about it when we meet.' It was the first thing I said to her.

My mother has always been deeply interested in my love life, always available to dish out some kind of advice (which always began with: 'In my time…'). I always debated and questioned the generation gap between us, telling her how she needed to stop using that phrase. It worked for some time, but not forever. It was monotonous and absolutely boring. My relationship with my mother is very strange. We are friends when it is convenient to be so, but we otherwise have a typical parent-child relation. But, all in all, I always confided in her about my dilemmas.

'Beta, relax. It's just been a month. Who is he?' I could sense that her imagination had already begun to act up, just from the tone I heard over the phone.

'Ma, you relax. It's not a big deal. I like this guy at school. He's doing a PhD in Medicine. We've just been hanging out a bit lately and he's been great. He's super knowledgeable and brings out the best in me; super supportive and ambitious and loving,' I went on and on, gushing about him.

'Beta, you must really like him. I've never seen you this way. Just be careful with everything. I don't want you to take any wrong steps or be trapped into a home that isn't even yours to begin with. Just take care, and remember, I love you,' she said, probably sobbing on the other side of the world.

I knew she really missed me.

'Ma, I miss you a lot. I know I don't call often, but you know I love you guys. I know it's been hard since bhaiya is also in Mumbai. I'll be done with this course in another nine months. I'll be back—really soon,' I tried to comfort her, even though I knew it barely made any difference.

It's just the harsh reality, I thought. *Our parents spend their lives working hard for us and trying to get us all the comforts and luxuries of life, just to see us smiling and happy, but in the path to achieving things in our own life, we end up detaching ourselves from a lot of things, including them. I know this is how life is but I wish there was some way to have it all. But that isn't life, is it? How can you have it all?*

'I know, my child, why worry? You focus on your studies properly and make us and yourself proud. I hope you've been writing well? Don't stop doing that, okay?' she said.

'Yeah, Mom, don't worry about me. It's been going well and will keep going well,' I assured her, bidding her farewell and hanging up. It had been a while since I had last spoken with Kabir, so I did my ritual and called him right after. We spoke at length and reminisced about the good times; we wished we could go back to the time when we were carefree. I missed him, my go-to person. It was difficult to not have him around, to not be able to see him for so long. Regardless, as he always used to say, 'Life goes on.' Life indeed went on, with or without certain people in it.

'Listen, are you done packing? I'm already feeling lost,' Ruchi said later that afternoon.

'What, already? No! We still have two whole days, Ruchi!' I exclaimed, laughing. Ruchi is the type to pack everything well in advance, remaining calm when others panic. But the process of packing itself made her crazy and paranoid. I was surrounded by unique people, I must say. Andrew is always calm, be it in any situation, while Lance made any calm situation full of excitement. Ally, on the other hand, gave no fucks—that's who she is as a person. She was still in the honeymoon period with her new British boyfriend. Ruchi was now momentarily crazy. And to think I used to be the one to be extremely excited and emotional about things. But it made us five a unique group. I had bonded well with them over time.

'Dude, it's in two days! Why aren't you excited, and how are you calm? Don't you have a submission tomorrow and don't you have to go shopping for the trip?' Ruchi exclaimed and I could see her eyes growing bigger and bigger in shock and anxiety.

'Bro, you need to chill the fuck out. And what's with your eyes? They're scaring me. I have already completed and submitted my paper well in advance. About shopping, I'll go tomorrow and shop. What's the big deal? Packing hardly takes fifteen minutes. I'll do it in the evening, tomorrow.'

'Okay, if you say so,' she said, pretending to not care. 'What about Ally, Andrew and Lance? Are they all ready?' she asked.

'I'd like to believe that. Relax. Is there something else going on, Ruchi? You don't seem normal. What's up?' I asked.

'No, no, it's nothing,' she said hesitatingly, and I figured that something was wrong. I didn't want to push her to say anything she didn't want to but I knew that something was going on with her. *She'll come around,* I thought to myself. Another voice snapped, *Okay, if you say so*. I was not convinced by either.

The next evening, I went shopping with Aryan. I had been keeping my relationship with him to myself. I didn't want people to know about him. Most people around me knew that I was dating some guy, but I never made anyone meet with him. I just did not want anything to get jinxed. Aryan and my relationship felt ideal, and I wasn't willing to compromise on any front. Aryan, being the sweetheart that he was, stayed by my side.

We shopped and had a good time. As we were getting back to the hostel, he dropped me off to my room. We both sat in there for a while in silence, until his hand rose to touch my face, and in less than a moment, I felt his lips on mine. It felt divine, and I had to close my eyes, and it kept happening. As his lips locked with mine, I could sense the calm in my heart. There wasn't any anxiety or any sort of nervousness, simply a sense of peace. It felt unreal, and I felt lucky that this was happening *to me*. I could feel his breath and his fragrance. Then he smiled and I couldn't help but blush and smile back. It wasn't a feeling that could be put into words. *My first kiss with him*. I felt like treasuring the moment, and somehow, I don't know what happened, but I felt a teardrop fall from the corner of my eye. Like this was the moment and the person I had been waiting for. He gave me a kiss on my forehead and it was time for him to leave, courtesy his PhD.

'Stay for a while,' I said, making a puppy face.

He hugged me and smiled, and we both curled up and lay down on the bed. We didn't speak a word, and it was only in the middle of the night that I woke up and realized that he was gone.

When did I fall asleep? I thought. Isn't it the best feeling to sleep peacefully in the arms of someone you love? *Did I just say love?* I must love him after all. Imagine that—meeting someone on the train in the strangest of ways, and then travelling all the way to Scotland to find them there. Isn't life very unexpected and strange? All the way from that train to Scotland—like destiny had had a hand to play. Who knew this would happen? Who knew I'd fall in love with the same guy I thought was the weirdest person I had ever met…

After he was gone, I reflected on my relationship with him. I did that quite a lot—reflect on things. Call it overthinking or over-analysis, but I had this bad habit of thinking too much about things.

I liked where things were going with Aryan. I even considered making him meet my parents after I'd return to India.

The night that he lay next to me as I fell asleep felt like it must have lasted for all eternity. It had never happened to me before. I had never fallen asleep without telling myself that I would now sleep. And there we were, just lying on the bed, no intention of sleeping, but I guess it had been so peaceful and divine in his arms. I wanted it to last. I wanted it to last so badly. In the span of a single month he had been able to create the magic I never thought I'd be able to experience. But there I was—living the experience itself.

It was 12.30 p.m., and late as it was, I thought I should get to packing finally. I was to leave the next evening. Fresh from my nap with Aryan, I wanted to get things done, otherwise I knew my eyes would be looking for him, my imagination only turning to him.

I packed my things and my bags were ready. The best thing about this trip was that I was also going to be able to see Aryan—and in Paris. I hadn't told my friends because they would have just gone mad and would have wanted to meet him, or possessively, would want me to spend time just with them. So, I dropped the idea of giving them a hint about Aryan being there as well.

I went to bed after packing with the memory still fresh. Believe me, even that happy thought worked to get a good night's sleep.

Next morning, I went to my class. I had a quick short test, which I was fully prepared for. I was glad about how I was handling things. Even though there was romance in my life, I never let it distract me from the other significant things in my life. I was able do it all, to focus on my studies and also spend time with my other friends. Aryan was always pushing me to study harder, and he constantly made sure that I didn't neglect my friends. He believed in prioritizing things in life, moment to passing moment, always telling me that it was important to derive happiness from different sources.

'Let happiness flow from different sources in your life. Allow it to happen. Don't block it,' he would say whenever I told him how he made me super happy. It felt like he was my friend, my love, my mentor, my guide—everything at the same time, and he was constantly pushing me to excel in various spheres of life.

After I had submitted my test to the instructor, I chatted with my classmates for a while. Most of my classmates were very hardworking, and I hardly ever saw them chilling. They were the super studious kinds. I was pally with some of them and often used to get tea or coffee in between lectures, but there was never an occasion to grow closer to them. And moreover, I felt content with the five people I had in my life.

I went back to the hostel and met Andrew, Lance and Ally. We were just getting ready to leave for the airport when suddenly we heard a scream from the building. In all the commotion, we ran out, only to hear that one of the girls had fallen from the fourth-floor balcony. It was horrible. We all rushed outside and waited until the ambulance came and took her away. Talk ensued after this, we learned that she was a science undergraduate student and it turned out that she had been pushed by her roommate. Her roommate had been taken along for an interrogation. It was so bizarre. We were shocked to the core, and we almost forgot that it was time for us to leave for the airport.

'It's so sad, and man, this isn't how we should start our trip. I need to make sure that she's alive. This is too horrific. I can't seem to stop imagining what might have happened,' I said, horrified and scared of what I had just seen.

'Okay, okay, we all need to calm down,' Andrew said, pulling out his phone. 'I'll find out somehow.'

'Okay,' I said, breathing with discomfort.

'I think we should just pray that everything will be okay,' Ally said.

We all took our bags downstairs to the main lobby. A lot of students had gathered there, those from other hostels as well. It was chaotic. Everyone was murmuring one thing or the other.

'This has never happened here before,' I heard one of the spectators say.

'I know, this is so damn horrific. You know, she was her friend. Apparently, there was some issue…something about a boy and they fought over it. So clichéd,' said another.

'Really? How stupid,' yet another one chimed in.

To me it just seemed like people were concocting stories of what might have happened. Nobody knew what had actually happened. In the meantime, Andrew was busy making some calls, and the staff were running around, trying to get the situation under control. There was suddenly a sad and scary vibe ringing throughout the entire hostel.

'Good news! She's fine. I mean, she will be fine,' Andrew said while running towards us. He must have heard from somewhere. 'She landed on her feet. The terrain was hard, so she broke her leg, and there are minor injuries on her head, but as per the doctors, she's going to be fine. She needs bed rest.'

'Oh, thank god!' I heaved a sigh of relief.

'What about the girl who pushed her?' Ruchi asked. She had come to stand next to us.

'Well, as far as I know, she's in custody and there's going to be some big case. As of now, she's with the police answering some questions, but it has been established that she did push her. The victim has also confirmed it. Her name is Angela,' he said.

'Oh, that is scary. How could people just do something like that, and that too to a friend?' I shuddered.

'Well, sometimes it's your friends who become your enemies, more than your enemies themselves,' Lance said out of nowhere. He was calm about it, as if lost in some thought or the other.

We all gave him a look. He saw us and shivered, as if he was creeped out by our stare.

'Don't worry, I am obviously not going to do anything to any one of you. I was making a point because it's a reality. Anyway, now that we know everything is going to be okay, should we leave for the airport?' he asked.

'I think we should leave. It gives us all the more reason to go for a holiday—away from this incident and all this negativity,' Ally said.

'Well, I think you're right. It's time to level up some positivity in life and enjoy—away from this hustle-bustle!' I exclaimed, finally managing a smile, even though deep down I was still unnerved, and everything seemed scary.

You don't really know anyone around you until you know them. You call someone your friend, and they turn out to not really be your friend at all. Sometimes situations bring out the worst in people; it isn't their true self. A situation makes them do things often out of their control—but killing someone or trying to kill someone—that requires a lot of courage and guts! What that girl had done sent shock waves everywhere. People had already started to question the foundations of their friendship, and I think they were probably doubting everyone around.

With these thoughts occupying me, we left the hostel and boarded an Uber to take us to the airport. We all had wanted this holiday, after all.

'I can't contain my excitement!' said Ruchi.

'Me neither,' Lance chimed in.

Everyone finally seemed to have composed themselves.

After an hour's drive, we reached the airport and completed all the formalities, rushing through them. We grabbed a bite even though the flight wasn't that long, but since we would reach Paris post dinnertime, we thought of eating something light. Both Andrew and Lance knew French—so it would be easier for us to roam around and experience Paris.

After we landed, we got into yet another Uber to reach our Airbnb. On the way, we saw the glowing lights of the Eiffel Tower and I couldn't contain my excitement. It was beautiful!

As we reached our Airbnb, my excitement only grew. It was a beautiful house, with a pool indoor and chairs set around; it had a vintage feel to it. The stairs were gilded, as if we'd entered the eighteenth century. The verandah was filled with many green plants and it filled the air with freshness and a pop of colour, making us glow the moment we entered our rooms.

The hosts were a gay couple with a child, one cute little boy.

They lived five houses away from the house that they were renting out to us; Andrew and Lance seemed to know them, which must have been why they had booked the place. Undoubtedly, it was heavenly. They had also engaged the services of a cook to help us with anything we wanted. The market was nearby and all the famous places were right across the street. The four-bedroom apartment was divided among us. Andrew and Lance took one of the rooms while we girls had one room each to ourselves. My room was filled with books and beautiful paintings on the walls, as if it had been designed especially for me.

We washed up and rested a bit. All of us were hungry so we decided to go out to eat somewhere near the Eiffel Tower.

Thanks to Andrew and Lance, communication was not a problem and we were able to commute very easily. As we reached the Eiffel Tower, all of us stopped talking, speechless at the sight of its beauty. The lights made it look heavenly.

We sat around and when we were about to leave, I asked my friends to go on ahead. I wanted to sit there longer by myself. But I was actually supposed to meet Aryan later; he had said he would come at midnight. At first, they refused. They did not want to leave me alone there, but I convinced them, telling them that our Airbnb was right across the street.

I sat there and closed my eyes to just take it all in. There's a reason why people call it the city of love. The air had love in it; the people seemed happy and the wind, blowing softly, made it an even more romantic place to be. As I was soaking it all in, I felt a light touch on my shoulder, a familiar and warm touch. It was Aryan. He kissed my forehead and sat down next to me to experience falling in love here, yet again. I don't know what happened but I said 'I love you' to Aryan right at that moment.

'Wow, Aveera, I love you too,' he replied with an insanely beautiful smile.

I couldn't help but kiss him with all my heart in it. The moment was straight out of a fairy tale and as clichéd as it sounds—there was the moonlight, the Eiffel Tower and the best man I could have asked for. As the roses blossom in the era of love and as the moon shines brighter on some days, just as the dewdrops in the early morning bring cool silence, it was something just like that, something that would make even the sun shine on the gloomiest of days. I was happy and content in that very moment, and there was nothing more that I could have wanted.

'How are you feeling?' he questioned as I enjoyed my moment in the sun.

'I feel good. I feel good about where we have come in such a short span of time, and I wish for it to last a lifetime,' I said. I knew it was a little too heavy, too much to utter in a fraction of a second but it was what I genuinely felt. I didn't see any point in keeping it to myself.

'I'm happy you do, Aveera. I feel happy too. This is nice and I'm glad we're here. Just enjoy the moment,' he said and smiled. The smile calmed me.

We sat there for an hour, eating an ice cream in the cold night of Paris. It's somehow more fun to eat an ice cream in the cold winter. It tastes even better.

'Let's go home,' I said and booked an Uber to my Airbnb. I knew everyone would be fast asleep and I could easily take Aryan with me. 'Yeah, let's,' he said and we started to walk towards our Uber, holding hands. We stayed entwined throughout the drive.

Back at the Airbnb, I slowly opened the door to avoid

disturbing anyone. We went upstairs, light-footed, straight into my room.

'Wow, this is a beautiful house and an even more beautiful room. Look at all these books! And it smells heavenly in here,' he said and I couldn't be happier, knowing he was also a reader and a creative person, apart from being the ambitious scholar that he was. The room had transformed into my safe haven and I didn't want to wish for anything different, neither in the person that I had in my life at that moment, nor regarding the city I was in.

I went to change and when I returned, he was already lying lazily on the bed. I jumped onto the bed and he grabbed me by my waist. His hands loosened my bun, which I had tied before leaving. He leaned forward and kissed me. His hands were at my waist, and as I felt the touch of his cold hands against my body, it sent shivers up my spine. I had goosebumps all over my body. I held him by his face as I got lost in the moment...

'You're very pretty,' he whispered into my ear. My face was turned to the other side of the bed as we cuddled peacefully. Around 3 a.m. I began to doze off, and he whispered, 'Good night.' I don't remember wishing him back until I woke up in the morning around 10 a.m. Lance knocking so loudly it could almost break my door.

'Dude, get the fuck up! Who sleeps until 10! Get up! We're going to be all touristy today. You can't afford to be sleeping all day, Aveera. I don't understand what you are doing. This is just not right. You need to get up and take a quick shower, get ready and leave or we are going to leave you at home,' he grumbled, continuously banging on my door.

'SHUT UP! Lance, I'm awake. Stop banging on the door,'

I shouted and opened the door only to see him still in his night suit.

'What the hell, Lance!' I said in a seemingly angry tone.

'Hahaha, sorry, sorry. I'm just changing too. I wanted to make sure that everyone was up and ready to leave in fifteen. You guys don't want to miss the cool art exhibition that they have organized at the Louvre,' he said.

'Okay, calm down,' I said and pushing him away from the door, jumped into the shower.

Having gotten dressed real quick, we decided to walk around the city instead of taking a cab or commuting. Lance was the first one downstairs, waiting for us in the living room. Ally and I packed some food with us, just in case. Ally had some food allergies, which is why we needed to be careful.

Paris was beautiful, an exquisite city. People were dressed as fashionably as I had always heard them to be. It was indeed the capital of fashion. Ladies with red lipstick and sharp stilettos, men with long coats, hats and cigars, old women rocking colours. I was quite intrigued and impressed by the styles everyone sported. Everyone seemed super active and pumped for their day. It was probably their active attire that made it seem that way.

I thought, *Isn't it true that when we are dressed properly, it gives us a different sense of confidence? I feel that way...*

We had a busy day ahead. As we reached the Louvre for the exhibition, I saw a couple getting a wedding video shot right next to it. They didn't care about the crowd gathered around; they were so engrossed in their moment that I felt like I was living through their day too. Having Aryan in my life made life so pleasant that I could relate to everything that was happening around me. I wanted something like that in my life.

'I love it! Just look at the art,' Lance said. He was really fond of art but the others were a little bored because art wasn't their cup of tea. I, on the other hand, was busy observing people and their actions. I liked observing and learning from little actions.

'You don't like art, Andrew?' I asked.

'Not all that much but Lance loves it so I always accompany him to all the exhibitions,' he replied with a smile, all the while looking at Lance who was busy grinning at some piece of art.

'Wow, that demands a lot of effort,' I said.

'No, not really. It's how you balance your time to do things for the people you love. I love him,' he said.

'What? Andrew, what did you say?' Lance asked, looking back in surprise.

I guessed that Andrew hadn't yet confessed his feelings to Lance. Andrew resisted the interrogation for a while, red in the face, but then he finally said, 'Oh my god, Lance. I love you. Yes, I really do and I'll go to as many exhibitions you want me to go to, as long as it's with you.'

I could see how hard Lance was trying to control his eyes from watering; the tears had already welled up.

'I love you too, Andrew,' he said, and they both kissed. All of us responded with an 'aww' in that moment. *Guess they found love in art, after all,* I thought. Their moment made our day better. Paris seemed even better.

'There's something else,' Lance said to Andrew.

'Tell me?' he asked.

'I don't want to make it seem real fast but I guess I want to stay here in Scotland after school is over, after all,' he said.

'What? Really? Lance! That'd be great. I love you. I love you,' Andrew said, almost giddy with joy and they kissed again. There must have been magic in the air. It was working for both of them so well.

And call it God's blessing or destiny, I saw Aryan checking out a painting, right across the street. I couldn't believe it. I was supposed to meet Aryan later at night near the Seine river. But I couldn't resist talking to him right there.

'Guys, you go ahead. I'm just coming. I'll meet you for lunch.' I said to my friends.

'Where are you going?' asked Ruchi, busy checking her makeup.

'Just there. I have to check two or three things here. Why are you fretting with you lipstick so much?' I asked. I knew there was something fishy going on, ever since we had left for the trip.

'Fine! I was trying to keep it a secret but I kind of found someone on Tinder,' she explained. 'I might have made this whole plan so I could meet the guy.' she said shyly.

'WHAT?' all of us exclaimed in unison.

'Dude, what's wrong with you?' I said, my eyes widening. I still kept an eye on Aryan.

'Stop judging. I'm supposed to see him today,' she said.

'All right, fine. It's fine, just be careful, all right?'

Everyone else seemed shocked.

'All right, guys. I'll see you in a bit,' I said, leaving the scene and walking towards Aryan, who had disappeared. I searched for a few minutes and finally saw him sitting on a bench with his eyes closed.

'Aryan?' I said, placing my hand on his shoulder.

'Woah, Aveera? How come you're here?' he asked with surprise written all over his face.

'I saw you, so came to say hi. I'm here with my friends. They've gone out for lunch, I'll join them there in a bit,' I said.

'Oh. How have you been? I've been missing you since last

night,' he said.

'Me too. When did you leave and why?' I asked.

'You don't want me to meet your friends, right? I had to leave, and my nana is in Paris too. I had to see her today,' he said.

'Oh. Do you want to meet my friends?' I asked.

'It's okay, Aveera. This is nice. I like the way things are, slow and steady and under wraps,' he said.

'Yeah, me too,' I said.

He gave me a peck on the lips. 'Come, let's walk around,' he said and held out his hand.

We walked and admired the art on the street. I seemed to like everything I saw. It was nice to be able to appreciate what the entire world had appreciated for so long.

'Aryan, can I ask you something?' I said, a little hesitation in my tone.

'Yes, love, tell me.' he urged.

'Where are you going to be after your PhD? It's a long course. What are your plans?' I asked.

'Aveera, I'm going to be in Scotland for a while. But I'll visit you—wherever you are. I love you and we'll make it work, regardless of where we are,' he said.

'Yeah,' I agreed.

'Why are you worrying? I gave you my word, Aveera. I haven't dated in a long time because everything fell apart the last time I did. And only after a lot of thought did I decide to go out with you. I ended up meeting you in the strangest of ways but I just want to be able to make you happy. I want us to grow—individually and together,' he said.

'Yeah, me too, Aryan,' I said with a smile.

'So don't worry. I'm right here and I'm going to be; always,' he said. I gazed at him and we kept walking. I rested my head on his shoulder.

'Okay, now you should go. Your friends must be waiting for you,' he said, breaking the spell.

'I completely forgot about that,' I said as I looked at my watch. It was late.

'Bye, take care. And be safe,' he said as he hugged me. 'I'll see you tonight?' I asked.

'Yes. See you.'

I rushed, navigating my way using Goggle Map. It's unlikely that I would have found the place without their services. It was a ten-minute walk from the Louvre. I hopped and skipped on my toes, my excitement clearly hinting to all that I was in love. People must have thought that I was mad—smiling all by myself, but then again, why would I care about what people thought? I was indeed in love! In love in the city of love!

'You guys, I think I really like art,' I said as I saw my friends sitting in this cute café, decorated with green plants.

'What took you so long, Aveera?' asked Ally.

'I'm sorry, I was engrossed in the art after all,' I replied, a half-lie.

'Yeah, sure,' Lance said, a little sarcastically.

'Hey, what was that?' I made a face.

'Nothing,' he said and started to dig into whatever he had ordered.

'I got you an avocado something, is that cool?' Ruchi asked me. I liked avocadoes so I thanked her.

Hungry, we all ate our food quietly, without looking up, when suddenly Ruchi exclaimed, 'Guys, he's coming here. OH!' she exclaimed.

'What? Why'd you call him here?' asked Andrew.

'It's apparently his favourite place to eat...you guys need to leave as soon as possible,' she said, worried he would see us.

'What? No no! We're staying. We won't say a word. You can use another table. I'm yet to finish my lunch,' Lance said, and all of us giggled.

'Come on, Lance. Don't do this. You found your love. Let me find mine,' she said.

'You can't find love like this,' he said, still eating.

Ruchi looked annoyed. 'Oh really?' she asked sarcastically.

'Yes, you don't have to go out of your way to find it. Let it come to you—naturally. Just keep it free and what's yours will find its way.' Lance explained what he meant. I wasn't sure, but there seemed to be some truth in it, at least for me.

Whatever is yours will find its way to you —one way or the other. Sometimes we spend our lives in pursuit of happiness, but it's only *after a while* that we realize that we need to let ourselves breathe. We need to let *that thing* grow with time, to let it come naturally to us. *Anything that's forced doesn't stay*, I thought.

I wasn't looking for love or anyone when I suddenly found Aryan. Life takes you places, in ways you couldn't have imagined. Maybe it was destiny playing its role in my life. Well, who knows? What mattered was that I was happy and content. I believed in destiny.

'Fine, I get it. But let me at least meet him now that he's here,' Ruchi said, eager to get away.

'Lance, stop troubling her. Let us go from here,' Ally said.

'It's okay, you guys can stay—just go sit inside,' Ruchi said, shooing us away with a gesture.

'Great, that works,' Lance said, excited.

We all moved our food and things inside the café, and we

saw Ruchi outside through the window, waiting for her mystery Tinder date.

We all gasped when we saw this really fair white guy approach and hug Ruchi. She saw us gaping from the corner of her eye and winked at us. She too must have been surprised by how beautiful that man was.

They were both sipping their tea in the cold weather when we suddenly saw the guy get up, agitatedly utter a few words, and leave. We were all confused about what had just happened between them. We all got up and went outside to check on her.

'Everything okay?' asked Ally.

'Dude, why did that handsome guy leave?' I asked. I didn't really care about what had just happened, why that guy had gotten so angry.

'Aveera, really?' Andrew said, exasperated with me.

'Sorry,' I stopped myself. 'What happened, Ruchi? Will you please tell us?' I asked again, this time with genuine concern.

'It's sickening how people can just come in and say whatever they like,' she said, annoyed.

'Arre, but tell us, what happened?' I repeated.

'He wanted me to go with him—to his house, and right away!' she explained.

'Oh.' Everyone sighed at this, except Lance, who spoke up. 'What else do you really expect, Ruchi, from such a sudden date?' he asked.

'Come on, she didn't know. So many people go out on Tinder dates,' said Ally, taking Ruchi's side and dismissing Lance.

'That's true actually. It's just a bad experience, nothing else. Don't worry. You'll meet a lot of people like him; they just have their own priorities,' Andrew said non-judgementally.

'Yeah. So it doesn't mean that you stop going out with

people, all right? It's fine, it happens. Just be careful about who you're going out with next time,' Ally said kindly.

Everyone was taking turns, trying to cheer Ruchi up, and I found myself lost in thought, *What if she had thought that he could be the one?* It's bizarre how all of us try to find love in one way or the other but turns out life isn't always all roses.

'It's fine, let's not spoil our trip over that moron. But it's good, at least we all came on this trip. We should thank him,' Lance said, winking at Ruchi.

'Hahaha, yeah…that's true,' I said and smiled. Cheered, we got up and left the restaurant. We were eager to resume the fun we had planned. We went to this cool bar near the Seine river. A very vintage place, with a rustic feel to it.

'Shots! Shots! Shots!' Lance sang as we entered the place. He was gone in a moment and I didn't even realize when he returned with several shot glasses. We had just entered the place. But I was enthused and I cried out in affirmation, singing along with him.

We all looked at each other, and with a loud 'Cheers!' downed our first shot.

After a few more shots, we started to feel the music. The music the pub was playing was soothing and we felt like we were swaying, like the wind; as if the music was specially being played for us. It was a very cosy and comfortable place. We were dressed casually, and felt comfortable that way.

A couple of guys were flirting with us, and to be honest, the attention felt good. We might have been tipsy or the guys were quite good-looking, but we enjoyed it. But all the while, I was constantly thinking about Aryan.

The DJ played a romantic song and all the couples came closer to dance with each other and in only a moment I found myself dancing with Aryan in that very bar! I didn't know where he had come from, but I didn't care. I immediately gestured to Ruchi and Ally to look towards me and see us dancing. They both smiled as I subtly pointed at him. I guess they liked him because Ruchi gave me that nod, with her eyebrows raised and her lips widening into a huge smile. *Was that approval?* I wondered.

All of us were in the zone and tipsy enough to enjoy the music and dance to it. We finally left the place around 12 a.m. for our hotel. I wanted to sit near the river with Aryan so I went ahead with him and asked the others to carry on. We all headed off in different directions. Lance and Andrew wanted to party a bit more so they stayed; Ally and Ruchi decided to go get some food. And I sat down near the river with Aryan. We held hands and said nothing for a long long time.

'I love you,' I said, my confession the first words in the moonlit night.

'I love you too, Aveera,' he replied and we kissed. I don't know how long we kissed but it was the most passionate kiss I had ever shared with him. Under the starry night, near the water under the beautiful sky, it felt amazing. Everything felt perfect. It felt like my love stretched from the sky to the waters, finally reaching the man in my arms. We talked for an hour—laughed, giggled, loved and comforted each other.

I later left to catch up with Ally and Ruchi. They were gobbling down food when I met them and Ally looked up at me. 'Listen, let's go for this Ferrari ride I have heard of,' she said. So we rented a car—a Ferrari—and had the most amazing drive of our life. It was crazy, the feeling of going faster than the wind.

I closed my eyes to take in the wind and the air, to feel it. The city kept getting better and better. It had so many experiences to offer. With music blasting in the car and the wind touching our body and minds, we felt absolutely free and light. You know the moment when everything's going well? It was that. That was the moment. It was an absolute state of serenity.

Who knew it was going to get better? When we finished our ride and left for the hotel, I heard snatches of Bollywood music near the Eiffel Tower and I couldn't control my feet. I lost myself and danced like there was no tomorrow. I bumped and danced and spoke with some really cool people there.

'Let's go, girls,' Ally finally said. 'And Aveera, you rock! What a carefree spirit you are.' And she hugged me.

'I love you girls,' I told them both and we slowly moved towards our Airbnb. It was four in the morning and we needed to sleep. Andrew and Lance were already in their beds, fast asleep, when we reached our Airbnb. The three of us crashed into our individual beds and passed out, like owls that had found time to rest after a whole night's vigilance.

The next couple of days in Paris passed by in a blur. I kept meeting Aryan and spending time with my friends, and soon enough, it was time to go back to Scotland. Andrew and Lance were carrying on with the trip, heading to Prague. The three of us finished up all we had to do and packed everything we had scattered. We went to the Eiffel Tower one last time and bid it adieu. It was time to head back to our home. Our little cosy hostel. I kept thinking about Aryan because I didn't know what his plan was, although I knew I was going to meet him in Scotland soon, even though it felt like we both were leaving behind memories in Paris. Whenever we'd come back, it would feel like we had just been there, just yesterday...

With these thoughts, we boarded our flight back to Scotland.

Six

The routine of our lives returned as we reached Scotland. We resumed our classes post our mini-break. The weather was getting colder day by day and it used to get dark way too early. The days felt too short and life was passing by rather quickly. We had our mid-term exams and submissions coming up and so we were all busy preparing. One could catch sight of students working hard everywhere.

I spent most of my time at the library. Aryan and I found our own, very silent corner and studied together there. It was going well.

It was amazing how well he supported me, especially regarding the work I had to do. When needed, he was there to guide me as a mentor, and when I needed him to be one, he was a friend. It was good to have him in my life.

'Are you ready for your exam tomorrow?' asked Aryan.

'I'd like to believe that,' I said with a little hesitation.

This was to be my first exam for the course, so naturally, there was a bit of tension regarding it.

'Don't worry, you're going to do great. Just breathe. It's all going to be okay,' he comforted me.

'Yeah, I'm sure,' I said and went into the exam hall to ace my first attempt. The two hours of the examination went pretty well. I was glad about how well I performed.

Time seemed to have slowed down during our examinations. Days took ages to pass. Studying as hard as we did, it might have had an effect on how we perceived time. With the passing of days, we came to the end of the exam season. Aryan was a huge support during the entire time: studying with me, motivating me, getting coffee when needed and helping with the late-night exam jitters—he handled it all quite well.

Everyone went home for their vacations after the exams. I accompanied Andrew and Lance to Iceland.

'This is a beautiful place,' I said the moment we entered Iceland.

'Indeed, it is,' said Lance.

We had booked an Airbnb near the cove, and the water was sparkling and blue, unlike anything I had ever seen before. It was magical: the vibe, the ice, the place—everything about it was magical.

At night, we decided to step out to experience the Northern Lights, if we were lucky enough to witness it.

'You want to know how we met?' Lance asked me.

'Yes, tell me. That should be interesting,' I said, already excited to know about their love story.

'We met in Australia. I was going on with my life, frustrated after I had quit my job. Normally, I just want to eat when I'm frustrated. I went to get some burgers and guess who was the cashier there?' asked Andrew with a smile.

'Lance!' I exclaimed. 'You were a cashier? Wow!' I said in a single breath.

'Yeah, yeah, I was,' he said shyly.

'I asked him for a burger and he messed up my order. Gave me an absolutely sad burger,' Andrew laughed.

'Yes, but you should be thankful that I did,' Lance said,

cutting Andrew mid-laughter.

'Okay, okay guys… Lance, let Andrew finish. You'll get your turn,' I said, interrupting their banter. Lance really wanted to play it cool.

'Yeah, so I complained to the manager about Lance. And oh, he indeed got an earful from the manager. I don't usually want to complain but I guess I wasn't in a good mood. I somehow projected my anger out onto him. But still, he did mess up my burger!' Andrew argued, looking towards Lance.

'Anyway, after that, he wrote an apology note to me—like a little kid. He offered to buy me a meal and a drink. But what happened next was pretty amazing. Lance started to cry after having offered the meal,' Andrew started laughing again.

'C'mon, do you really have to bring this up?' Lance said, almost crying again.

'Don't be upset, man. I think that was kind of cute,' said Andrew and held Lance's hand. They both shared their characteristic smile again.

'Okay, fast; you can do your romance later, guys,' I said, now intrigued and interested in knowing what happened next.

'So yeah, he cried and I felt so bad. But the truth was that Lance had lost the only watch he had, which is why he was upset and lost the whole day. I found it quite cute and I asked him out. I took him out to buy him a watch and there began our love story—with that watch I bought,' Andrew said.

'Guys, that *is* cute,' I said, not really meaning it. But it was cute to see them like this, glad that they found it cute. They found happiness in the little things in life and that only made the bigger events even more worthwhile.

We ate some food later, and we decided to try and see the Northern Lights again, having failed the last time a few hours ago. From what I have heard, it's a one-time experience, something every person should try once in their life.

Call it destiny or a blessing, we got to experience the Northern Lights on our first night itself. Sitting in the dark night, looking up at the sky playing with the lights, was the best thing I have experienced in a long long time. The three of us were quiet for the longest time, admiring the beauty we were surrounded with.

In a nutshell, we're all made up of the particles nature has offered us; the most peace we have is from nature itself. It is very important to sit back and enjoy the beauties and bounties of this earth, to spend time with oneself, reflecting on the kind of person we've been and want to become. I looked at the sky as if it were telling me a story. The green aurora lights in the sky were jumping from angle to angle, and it had created such a beautiful atmosphere. The dark night was lit up with the green colour of prosperity. *Imagine, nothing stays dark forever. There's always a window of some light in one way or the other,* I thought. *And I just found that light right above me in nature.*

'Lance, listen…' said Andrew, breaking the silence as he got up from the spot we were lying in to look at the sky.

'Yes, Andrew…' he said, getting up as well.

And Andrew bent on one knee as I gazed at the two in amazement. 'Will you marry me?' he asked Lance.

Lance and I looked at each other, and I saw Lance had tears in his eyes.

'Andrew, oh my god. Yes! I love you! I will marry you,' he said, the words tumbling out all at once.

They both hugged and shed some tears. I think they kissed for the longest time. I kept looking at them and looking away, a mute spectator. I couldn't help but realize that I was crying too.

I think, by far, it was the most adorable thing I had ever seen. I missed Aryan at that point but I was too happy for Andrew and Lance to think about Aryan for a long time.

'It seems like you made us come on this whole trip for this, no?' I asked Andrew.

'I have been carrying this ring for a while now, but I was waiting for the right moment and I didn't want to wait for it any longer. I always knew he was the one,' he replied shyly.

'The one!' How do you know who the one is anyway? I thought. When is it that you decide or come to know that he/ she is the one? We have created this bubble around us about the kind of person we want to love or who we want to be with, but truth be told, we don't know anything. When that bubble bursts, we shatter...

'Congratulations guys, I am so happy for you,' I said.

'Don't worry, you'll find someone who is just right too, Aveera,' Andrew said with a wink, teasing me about Aryan, whom he still hadn't met.

We all went for dinner and the next day I had decided I would give them space and so, I didn't third wheel with them. I roamed around the town and had this amazing time by myself. My life seemed complete at the time because I was happy. I was carried away by this feeling of peace and fulfilment. I felt positive energy from all spheres around; everyone was in love, I was surrounded by happy people and it was a beautiful feeling. Things were in place for me.

After having spent another day in Iceland, it was time for us to head back to Scotland. I was full of anticipation about meeting Aryan. After all the romantic experiences we had in Iceland, it made me feel super excited to see Aryan. It had been quite a while since I had last seen him.

'Let's go, let's go, let's go,' I chanted with enthusiasm to Lance and Andrew.

'Slow down, Miss. What's the hurry? We are not missing our plane here,' Lance said, joking as he hurried up.

'Yeah, what's up?' asked Andrew.

'Nothing, I just wanted to go back to a place that isn't as cold,' I said, trying to hide my excitement.

'All right, I hope there's nothing else,' Lance said in a wicked tone. Andrew gave me a smile; he had probably figured out that I was excited about meeting the man I had been secretly seeing. The good thing about Andrew was that he never shared secrets with other people. He was a good secret keeper. He never told anyone about my anxious moments and my love for Aryan to anyone else, not even Lance, which was kind of a relief.

We boarded the plane for Scotland and I couldn't be more excited. As we walked out of the terminal, I saw Aryan standing at the airport gate, waiting for me. I was so excited that I wanted to run right into his arms and hug him real tight. Andrew and Lance were behind me, so I waited.

'Guys, you go ahead. I'll be behind you,' I asked.

'Okay, we'll see you at the hostel,' Lance and Andrew nodded in agreement. They both left for the hostel as I waved, then I went running towards Aryan, who was still standing at the side. We kissed and it felt like it had been too long since I had last seen him. I guess Iceland had made me fall in love with him even more, and I don't know why, but I just wanted to marry him—right then and there, to feel the same feeling that Lance and Andrew shared. I was just thinking about all this, lost in the kiss, when suddenly, Aryan was on his knees.

'Aryan?' I uttered with shock, surprise and emotions I had never even felt before.

'Will you marry me, Aveera?' he asked.

'Oh Aryan! Yes! Yes, I will marry you. But…are you sure? It's only been a while…'

'I know. Sometimes it's not about the time but about the person, Aveera. I don't think I'll ever be more compatible with anyone else—not the way I am with you,' he said.

Have you seen a rose bloom? Yes, a rose. It felt like there were thousands of roses blooming in my heart. The feeling couldn't be more priceless. I was in love and things were just falling in place, just the way I had been thinking. I had the best life had to offer.

'I love you, Aryan. And yes, I will marry you, with all my heart,' I replied, with tears falling from my eyes. Aryan hugged me really tight and we celebrated the love we shared for each other. Things were happening the way I wanted them to! I was going to get married to the man I loved. With only a few months left for me to complete my master's, I couldn't wait to get back home and prepare for the next journey of my life.

'Let's go?' asked Aryan and held out his hand.

'Yeah,' I said, all startled and still lost in my thoughts. We left for the hostel. We both were silent the entire way. But the ride was beautiful, with so many emotions and so many unspoken words echoing inside us. I had to tell my parents. Even though I kind of felt positive and was sure of them accepting Aryan, I was still nervous. We got out of the cab and started to walk towards our hostel.

'I'll be right back. See you in the evening?' he asked.

'Okay, I'll see you,' I told him. I saw him walking away from me with a smile. My heart felt the warmth it had not felt in the longest time. I closed my eyes, took a deep breath and started walking.

In no time, a car rammed into me. I could see my life going away from me. With the swooshing noise, everything seemed to slow down. I had tears in my eyes as I fell on the road, blood gushing around me. Everything was hazy, and with no energy left in me, I gasped and uttered a last cry, calling out to Aryan.

Seven

Rishika

It seemed as if the earth had almost slipped away, right beneath my feet. The news of Aveera's accident while at Scotland had shaken everyone. There was chaos, fear and panic at her house when I visited.

'We need to go to Scotland as soon as possible,' Reena aunty, Aveera's mother, said.

She was inconsolable. Everyone in Aveera' family was tense. Everyone kept breaking into sobs and curses, except Aveera's father, Manoj uncle, who was extremely quiet.

'We'll have to get her here. She's getting operated right now—that is all we know,' Reena aunty continued.

'Yes, yes, we will get her back, but first you need to control yourself,' Manoj uncle said.

He was arranging tickets for himself and Reena aunty. They had to get Aveera back to India.

'Rishika, just make sure you keep checking in on her through her friends there. Do you have their numbers?' he asked me.

'Yes, uncle. Don't worry,' I said. 'I'll do my part.'

'No wonder you are her best friend,' he said and hugged me. I couldn't help but shed a few tears. Aveera's family was just like my own family and to see them all in this state made my heart weak. But I had to keep them all strong.

'Don't worry uncle, she will be fine,' I said and tried to comfort them. But I didn't know how to—I mean, it's beyond words how they must be feeling—their child away in a foreign country, struggling to hold on to her life in a hospital they couldn't reach yet.

'I'll drop you guys to the airport,' Aveera's brother Tej said.

'Yes, let's go,' Manoj uncle said, as they hurried to catch the flight to Scotland.

Meanwhile, in Scotland…

'Why did we leave her alone at the airport?' Lance said, crying and hugging Andrew.

'She will be fine,' Andrew said, trying to calm Lance, and himself, down.

'How do you expect us to calm down?' Ally cried. 'It isn't a situation that can be controlled.'

'Doctor, please tell us how Aveera is?' Ruchi asked at the first sight of a doctor in a coat.

'It's too soon to say, Ma'am. Please be seated. We'll let you know about any progress. Are her parents going to be here soon?' he asked.

'Yes. They are on their way. But why do you say it's too soon to say?' Ruchi asked, alarmed.

'Ma'am, it takes time. Please let us do our work and we will let you know everything,' he said and went inside, faster than the wind, leaving the four more anxious than they had been before.

The situation did not look good and the tension in the air was increasing. Aveera had been in the ICU for the longest time now, and there was no clarity about her well-being. It felt like someone had stabbed the four friends in their hearts. Aveera was a ray of sunshine in their lives, constantly uplifting others and making sure all her friends and, her family was happy. In fact, she was a positive ray in every life she touched. The entire hostel was talking about her. Everyone was worried. The driver of the car that had rammed into Aveera had been arrested, but his arrest would only do so much; for everything else, they had to pray. If only there was a way to bring Aveera back…

The four remained at the hospital the entire day and took turns bringing food for everyone else. Aveera's parents were going to be there soon, and they would have to hold the fort till then.

'Ma'am, you should go home. Maybe one person can stay. This will take some time,' the doctor said to Ruchi.

'We're all staying here, Doctor. Don't worry about us,' replied Ally.

'Yeah, don't worry. How's Aveera doing? Is there any improvement? Her parents are arriving today and we want to be in a position to tell them something positive,' Andrew said.

'I'm sorry, but I cannot say anything yet. A lot of blood has been lost.' the doctor said and hurriedly left for the ICU. Things didn't seem to be fine. The doctor sounded calm, but was it only the calm before the storm? Lance, as always, seemed extremely anxious and worked up. Andrew, on the other hand, was trying to calm him down and was making everyone see things positively, hopefully.

'Yes, yes, this is the hospital,' said Ruchi, constantly on the call with Rishika. She had called Aveera's parents and had given them Ruchi's and Ally's phone numbers as well, for them to be able to find the four friends when they reached the hospital.

'We've reached beta, we're going to the hospital now. We'll call you as soon as we have something,' Manoj uncle told Rishika.

'Okay, sure, Uncle, I'll be waiting to hear from you as soon as you reach,' Rishika replied.

Rishika

I don't know why such a thing happened to Aveera; she has already seen so much in her life, an accident seemed absolutely uncalled for—she didn't deserve it. She had seemed so happy in Scotland and to hear of her suffering now broke my heart. I didn't want to wait so helplessly in India.

I heard the clouds thundering outside and it seemed like it was going to rain heavily. I had the urge to go to Scotland myself, to see what was happening, to be by my friend's side. I checked with my parents and booked the next flight, making sure to inform Aveera's parents on the way to the airport.

I wanted to reach the hospital as soon as possible. After a good nine hours of constant worrying, I landed at the hospital. I couldn't wait to see Aveera, to hear some positive news. I called Aveera's friend, Ruchi, checking where they all were waiting. Ruchi and her friends were still all at the hospital, sitting with Aveera's parents. After about an hour, I reached the hospital and straightaway rushed towards Aveera's parents. From a distance I saw Reena aunty crying, and Manoj uncle trying to calm her down.

'Aunty! How are you? How is Aveera?' I asked her, hugging her to give her comfort and ground myself.

'Doctors are still not saying anything. She's been monitored in the ICU for a while now, and…I'm really scared,' she said, trying to wipe away her tears.

'Beta, you didn't have to come all the way. We would have informed you,' Manoj uncle said.

'No, Uncle, I just couldn't stay there. What are the doctors saying?' I noticed a quiver in my voice. I wasn't sounding strong, and I didn't want to break down in front of her parents.

'There's no news yet. There's a lot of loss of blood. That's all we know,' he said.

'Okay,' I calmed myself down and went to sit on the bench with Reena aunty. I saw Aveera's friends approach. 'Hi, I am Ruchi. This is Lance, Andrew and Ally,' Ruchi said, introducing everyone.

'Don't worry, Aveera's going to be fine,' Andrew said to me. His tone was calm, just as Aveera used to say it was. It made me feel peaceful.

'If you guys want to go home and rest, please go ahead. I'll be here with aunty and uncle,' I said, concerned about all of them. They had been there for about a day and a half and they all look sleep-deprived to me.

'No, we'll be here until we hear something from the doctors,' Lance said, and everyone else nodded in affirmation. They seemed to have made up their minds, so I didn't say anything more.

I guess everyone was sailing in the same boat; all of us prayed together, waiting to just talk to Aveera again. The lack of information and the long wait had settled into a gloomy silence and we sat there, drifting into different thoughts, waking every now and then in fear and apprehension. This continued till the doctor came up to us. 'Sir, may I please have a word with you?' he asked, gesturing with his hands.

'Yes, please…please tell me…please,' uncle replied; that was when I realized how helpless he must be, how hard he had been taking it. He was begging to hear something positive.

Yes, Sir. Please come with me,' the doctor said. Manoj uncle and the doctor went into the room adjacent to us. We didn't know what was really happening. But in a few minutes, I saw uncle coming out of the room, his eyes full of tears. He could no longer hold them back. He came and hugged Reena aunty. There was silence. Everything seemed still, an absolute vacuum. Our heart skipped a beat. I just wanted uncle to tell us what the doctor had told him, and quickly.

'She's in a coma,' he said finally, without beating about the bush. Then he broke down.

Waves of shock washed over all of us, leaving us without words. I couldn't comfort anyone, and felt my eyes well up. I was wiping away my tears but the pain was mind-numbing. Just a few days ago, Aveera was this happy, chirpy person, and suddenly, she was in a coma! Reena aunty was numb. She wasn't crying any longer. I could sense her fear but she didn't say a word.

'Reena, we'll pray hard and our daughter will come back to us. Don't worry Reena,' Manoj uncle said, even though he was crying himself. He wanted to ensure that Reena aunty was comforted. And suddenly, I heard her crying as well.

'My daughter…my child…my love,' she howled; almost everyone in the hospital felt her pain.

'Reena…Reena…she will be fine,' Manoj uncle hugged her.

'Aunty, I promise she will be fine. She has to be fine,' I said, trying my best to calm her down, but she wasn't really consolable. I was speaking to fill the silence and didn't expect her to be consoled after having heard that her child was in a coma. All of Aveera's other friends were trying to console themselves, while talking to Manoj uncle. Everyone was in shock.

'We should have come with Aveera from the airport,' Lance said, crying and hugging Andrew.

'It's okay Lance, do not blame yourself. Aveera will be fine. We'll go to church today. She's going to be okay,' replied

Andrew, but he too had tears in his eyes. The entire world had come crashing down and it seemed difficult for us to bear such heaviness.

Meanwhile, Manoj uncle went inside with the doctor to check on how we should proceed with things. It was a difficult time for the entire family and the friends and I still had no idea about what had actually happened.

'Rishika, can you please check the tickets? And also ask about special medical services for the journey,' uncle asked when he returned. He was fulfilling all the formalities with the hospital needed for Aveera's travel back to India. Reena aunty seemed to have crumpled in a corner.

'My daughter, please talk to me...' she kept crying.

Aveera was still inside the ICU.

'Doctor, what exactly is the situation, please, can you tell me?' I asked, needing to hear for myself.

'She's in a comatose state. Her brain is working; she can see and hear whatever is happening around her, but because of the shock and the internal damage, she cannot talk. Her body is paralysed. In such cases, patients generally recover at some stage, but we cannot really determine when that will happen. You just need to be active in front of her. Try and make her smile. Don't worry, pray for the best,' the doctor replied.

'Can I go see her?' I asked.

'Yeah, sure. Just try not to cry,' he patted my shoulder and warned me, concerned.

'Yeah,' I replied, and with a sigh I went in, afraid of what I would see.

I saw Aveera lying on the bed, looking up at the roof. Her hands lay still at her side. Her head was bandaged well to cover up all the injuries. I walked slowly towards her. She hadn't noticed my presence, and I desperately wanted her to. Her right foot had dressing on it, and there was more on the left knee. The hospital room was very well maintained. Aveera's eyes were turned towards me but they were blank, devoid of feeling or recognition. She didn't say a word, didn't express anything. She was empty. The world felt empty and I wanted to cry. She was my best friend.

I went and sat near her.

'Hey, you're going to be all right very soon. We're all going back home. I am sure you will love it back home,' I said, waiting for her to at least blink in affirmation. But she didn't respond. She didn't react. She was motionless. I had never seen her like this. I couldn't hold back my tears. The entire paranoia, the rush, the emotions, everything just rushed out of me in loud sobs. Without saying another word, I rushed out, hiding my face with my hands. Ally and Ruchi came running towards me and hugged me.

'Hey, it's okay. She's going to be fine. Don't cry. The doctor asked us to stay calm, remember?' said Ruchi.

'I just can't see her like this. She's always such a happy bird; seeing her in this state pains me,' I said, wiping my tears.

'I know, she was just having such an amazing time in Iceland with Lance and Andrew and suddenly she's in there—unable to say a word, or even move,' Ally said.

'Yeah, but we need to be strong. You guys are flying to India tomorrow. I'll help you figure everything out. Come…' Ruchi said, and holding on to my arm, took me along with her. I saw aunty give me a helpless look. I looked back with a half-confident smile. We comforted each other by sharing our pain, communicating with our eyes. We had to be strong for Aveera.

Manoj uncle's phone was constantly ringing, relatives calling in from India and checking on Aveera. He calmly spoke to each of them, but I could see how he struggled. We stayed the night in Scotland and booked a flight for the next morning at 11 a.m. Special medical services were to be provided for Aveera for her safe journey.

Next morning, we took our luggage and I bid goodbye to all of Aveera's friends in Scotland. They all bid goodbye to Aveera, even though Aveera still had nothing to say to them, not even give a glance of awareness. There were tears all around.

'I'll visit India soon,' Ruchi said to me finally.

Ally joined in and said, 'Yeah, me too. In fact, all of us will come.' Lance and Andrew nodded in affirmation. I smiled and nodded back.

'Bye, take care. I'll keep you guys posted,' I said with a wave.

Lance was still in tears, still upset about the fact that they had left Aveera alone at the airport. It wasn't his fault, I thought.

'Aveera, we're going to India,' I said, knowing she wouldn't react but I still hoped she would say something or at least make a gesture, but it was in vain. Her eyes were blank.

Medical assistance arrived as we reached the airport. Reena aunty stuck by Aveera's side and was with her throughout the journey, despite the argument with an official or two. Aveera's brother was supposed to be at the airport gate to pick us all up. We all managed to reach Delhi without crying out loud. As soon as we reached Delhi, Tej bhaiya was there, and broke into tears as he hugged Reena aunty. It must have been tough to stay back in India and only hear what was happening in Scotland.

He saw Aveera and said to her, 'Oye, I won't trouble you, I promise, but at least reply na. Say something to me Aveera... don't do this. You want all that money I said I'll send on Rakshabandhan? I'll give it to you now. Tell me what you want to buy, I'll buy it for you, but please…please…say something,' and broke down. I had never seen him cry before, but he couldn't control himself and seeing him, tears fell from my eyes as well.

'Tej, control, beta, you need to be strong for her. The doctor has asked us to smile and be happy in front of her. Be patient. She is going to be okay. We just have to ensure that she's taken care of, Tej,' Manoj uncle said, trying to comfort him with a rare hug.

'Yeah,' he said and went up to get the van for us, along with the medical assistance team from our hometown.

I had imagined that Aveera would be coming back soon, she would have graduated and I'd have come to pick her up. It would have been all happy and gay. But the situation today was so distant from that thought, so grim. We all got into the car and the journey ahead of us seemed to be full of gloom. I was looking at Aveera, hoping for her to just get up suddenly and say something.

We reached Punjab after four hours and my parents were there to meet all of us. They looked just as worried as everyone else, their smiles crumbling when they saw how difficult it was for me. As we got out of the van, I felt for a moment as if Aveera had spoken, but it was just my imagination.

'Beta, you go home now, we are here to take care of Aveera. The nurses are also going to be around. You don't need to worry. I will call you in case there is something, and especially if there's any progress from Aveera's end,' Manoj uncle told me.

'Yes, Uncle. Please call me when you get to know something,' I said. I really needed some rest. We stopped at Aveera's house for half an hour, as my parents conversed with Manoj uncle and Reena aunty, asking them to let us know in case they needed anything, telling them that we'd pray for the best.

'Aveera, recover soon. Your best friend will go crazy otherwise. I will make your favourite pasta when you come,' my mother kindly said to Aveera. I became teary-eyed when she said that. I really really wanted Aveera to get well as soon as possible. I just couldn't do anything for her and the feeling of helplessness was killing me.

'Hey, bye…I will come soon; please talk to me when I come back. Enough of all this now, okay?' I told Aveera sternly. She was looking directly into my eyes, as if she really wished to respond, but was unable to do so.

We left soon after.

As soon as we reached home, I planned to go back after a few days, to stay with Aveera and help around the house for a week. I took a leave from work. It wasn't just friendship; Aveera was like my sister. She was there with me and for me throughout our childhood, always making the day brighter. I'd never even seen her grow bitter; she would manage her anger and sadness and vent it out on her own, or cry it out to me, and then, she would become her old self, as if nothing had ever happened. I just wanted to ensure that she would be fine. I wanted to stay as positive as possible for her, just as she had been for us, for all of us. I just wanted her to be fine.

But a month passed by, and I still couldn't get Aveera to respond. It was getting harder than we all had thought it would be. I don't even know if she felt anything.

Eight

Aveera

How do I explain this to you? I understood everything. I knew what was happening around me. It was a bit hazy so I couldn't grasp everything. But I could see that I was in India, in my home. I didn't feel anything though. I didn't know how to react; the world seemed still. I could see people touching me, and I could see them cry. I really wanted to tell them that I loved them. I wanted to feel things. I wanted to hug my mother, my father, but I couldn't move my arms. And every now and then, there was a haze. I couldn't really see what they all were doing around me; their voices were distorted and their faces seemed bigger than ever. I wasn't able to react. But where was Aryan? Did anyone even inform Aryan? Did he know I was in India?

My mind quietened and I couldn't feel a thing.

'Aveera, listen to me. I know you can hear me, and I know you will recover, beta. Nothing has happened to you. Your entire family is there with you. We're going to dance with joy like you always used to do, and we are going to make sure that everything else falls into place, just right. Rishika will come here too; she's been great. All of your friends from Scotland, they'll come too,' my mother said and I tried to put two and two together about what she was really saying.

When she talked about my friends visiting from Scotland, I immediately thought about Aryan. Since Ruchi had already seen me with Aryan, I thought she'd informed him and Aryan must have contacted Ruchi. I just hoped he'd come too. I missed him. Everyone I loved was around me, but he wasn't. I wanted to speak to my mother, and say, 'Ma, I love you. I know I am going to be fine. But Ma, I feel helpless, Take me out of here. I want to talk and feel things again.'

If only my mother could hear me… But all I could do was observe the things happening around me. I could do nothing about them. I don't even know if I felt pain, but I certainly felt the heartache. All I wanted to do was to talk to them, to talk to each person who was trying to say something to me. All I wanted was for these people to be around me. Mom was always there, and the nurses were constantly hovering around. I felt my energy had drained and then, I felt feeble. The movement of the fan in a circular motion was the only thing I noticed. It was the month of March, I think. The fans were on. I could see everyone around me sweating. But there wasn't really anything I could do.

Rishika, too, had come to see me and stayed by my side. 'Aveera, all your friends from college are here,' she said and I could see faces I knew so well. My best friend, Kabir, was there, teary-eyed, and all my other friends were there too. I could see them saying something, but I couldn't really gather what they were trying to say. It was too much. Then I heard Kabir say, 'Aveera, I love you. Now get the hell up and talk to me.'

I love you too Kabir. So much that I can't explain, I wanted to say.

'C'mon, we were going to come to Scotland and you have already come back. This isn't fair, Aveera, at least get up and take us to Scotland,' said Poonam, another friend.

I wish I could take you to Scotland, I thought without saying anything at all. But what had happened to me? I didn't remember much. How did I even land up here?

I didn't really know what had happened before I noticed being at home. I couldn't seem to recall anything. I had got off the cab! There, I remember that. Everything else seemed so hazy. I wanted to scream. I wanted answers from somewhere, someone.

'Aveera, you know, even your friends from Scotland are going to visit you in a few days,' said Rishika.

I really wanted to meet them... Wait...stop. The nurse was doing something to me. I was talking to Rishika in my mind when the nurse came to inject me with something. I wanted her to stop so I could talk to my friend, ask her if Aryan was coming as well. And I wanted to know about the paper I had submitted. Did I do well? I wanted to get it published. I wanted to know...

I don't know what happened, but it felt like I had fallen asleep, but I wasn't awake yet. There were flowers all around me and I could only see Kabir there. I felt a teardrop fall from my eyes. Suddenly Kabir jumped up, 'Nurse, nurse! Aunty. Tej! Guys, come in, please fast...guys!'

He was shouting loudly and I could see a lot of faces close to mine.

'Nurse, look, I just saw a teardrop fall from her eye,' Kabir said to the nurse. 'I think she's listening to us and she can feel things,' he said in excitement.

'Aveera, Aveera, my baby. How are you? My bacha, talk to me Aveera,' my mother said, placing her hands on my shoulders.

'Ma'am, Ma'am, please don't do this. It's a good sign that

she is feeling a little but don't be impatient and don't touch her like this. It will give her a shock—and you do not want that. So please everyone, please just take it slow. Let the patient breathe properly and don't make it harder for her,' the nurse said, and then asked my mom to move away a few steps.

Well, the nurse was doing her job, even though I had wanted my mom to come and sit near me. She had been crying for so long and I just felt like I could feel her warmth, just a little. My emotions almost burst out of me. Even though I wanted to cry, I couldn't really. I wanted to hug them all and cry.

'Aveera, listen, we all love you. You're going to get up soon and you are going to feel everything. Aveera. Your friends from Scotland are also going to be here soon. I can't tell you how happy I feel. I love you. I really really love you, Aveera,' Kabir said and held my hand. It was warm, it was good. Neither he nor I had ever talked about what we shared because we wanted to have a relationship that did not require a tag. It was so warm, so good to have someone care for you so much. Besides, he knew I was seeing a guy who made me happy and complete, and he was the happiest when he got to know that. And at the moment, I wanted to hold his hand and tell him that I loved him too. I knew I was going to be fine and going back to Scotland and to everything. I wanted to get things back to normal.

They all sat and chatted near me. I was able to gauge some of the things they said, and I couldn't make sense of some things, but I knew that I was indeed going to get better soon. It was difficult to make sure when that would happen, but I felt the warmth all around me.

'Listen, Aveera, I am going to be back soon okay,' said Rishika, and I wanted to hug her in that moment. From what

I think, she's been constantly there beside me. I don't think I've had any better friend than her, no one who's crossed so many bridges for me, so many times. She was my best friend. She was family.

I blinked my eyes in response and she stood still in amazement, breaking into a dance as she realized what had happened.

'Nurse! She blinked; she blinked as if she just nodded,' she said to everyone.

'Yes, Ma'am. A few more days and she will be able to move and do things normally. Just give it some more time,' said the nurse. Everyone had a cheerful smile on their face and tears of joy. I could see it but I still couldn't say anything. Not yet.

I saw Rishika leave, while everyone else got busy with their own merry-making. My eyes met my mother's, she was telling my father about what had happened and there was so much purity in her smile and in her eyes. Is there anything above your parents' love?

'She blinked and she can now feel things,' my mother said to my father over the phone. and I was sure he was telling her that he couldn't wait to come home and see it for himself. I was my dad's favourite, or so I believed. I knew he would always hold my hand and face any problems that would come my way, standing right next to me. I felt hopeful at that moment.

I was waiting for everyone from Scotland to come and be with me, and for Aryan to finally, finally meet me. I missed him. Everyone else was there but my friends from Scotland and Aryan.

A few days passed by. People continued to visit and it was getting monotonous and my heart longed to meet Aryan. I could feel the pain I carried in my mind and my heart. And it was even more frustrating that I couldn't move. Life was very hollow, but full of emotions that were ready to explode. The worst part was that I wasn't recovering as fast as I wanted to. One afternoon, I saw my mom crying, 'Get up now my bacha, please, it's been long enough. You're scaring me,' she said. And I couldn't say a word.

Mom, I can hear you. I want to get up too, Maa. I can't help it, Maa. What do I do, Maa? What do I do? Please help me, Maa. Please, I wanted to scream. I wanted to cry. My body was not responding to anything.

'Nurse, when will she get better? What is going on? Just last week, she was able to feel and listen to us. She even shed a tear, but nothing more seems to be happening. The doctor told us that normally a patient takes about a week to get back to their normal state but nothing is happening right now. Please tell us, what should we do?' my crying mother asked the nurse.

'Madam, please don't worry. Every case is different. We hope she will get her body movement and senses back very soon,' she said, consoling her.

'Hoping? What do you mean hoping? Can it get worse? Tell me clearly right now,' said my mother, angry as well as sad.

'Ma'am, please. You need to relax. We want her to get better as soon as possible. As I have told you, each case is different. I cannot say anything for sure. You just need to stay positive and keep talking to her. The more positive the atmosphere around her is, the better are her chances,' the nurse replied in a calm tone.

Meanwhile, my dad came in and tried to calm my mother. 'Reena, don't worry. I am telling you, she's going to be fine. Let's pray to God for her speedy recovery.'

'And you, my dear daughter Aveera,' he turned to me. 'We have so much to do together. All our plans of co-writing a book, remember? So, you better get up real quick and get to work because there's a lot to be done.' I wanted to smile when he said that. My dad and I shared a beautiful bond. We had this plan to write a book together; it had been our plan for a long time. I had been so caught up with my social life that I didn't spare any time for him. I would definitely make some time for him when I am better. I was hoping that I would feel better really soon. I was still hopeful.

My friends from Scotland were going to be in Punjab. I heard my mother invite them the next day. I was actually thrilled to get to see all of them. In such a short span of time, I had made such good friends. Ruchi, Ally, Lance and Andrew were my family in Scotland. And, of course, the love of my life—someone I was looking forward to meeting for a long time, whom I met in Scotland. He made my life complete. I couldn't wait to see him. I dozed off intermittently as I lay in bed, and when I next opened my eyes, I could see their beautiful faces around me. At first, it was all hazy, but soon I could see Ally, Andrew, Lance and Ruchi sitting around me and the nurse holding something near my arms.

I wanted to scream, *I missed you so much.*

'Oh my god, Aveera, I missed you so so much. I wish I had taken you back from the airport along with me,' Lance said, teary-eyed.

'Hey Lance, remember—no crying.' Andrew politely asked Lance to wipe away his tears, which, of course, eventually Andrew himself did, reaching out to touch his face. My cutest couple was with me again.

'Aveera, how are you? You're missed in Scotland. India is beautiful. Are you going to get up and show us around like you told us you'd? That has to be quick. We have a break now, so we're going to be exploring India with you,' Ally said.

Before she could finish, Andrew added, 'Well yeah, that's the plan she made. She cannot ditch us now. Aveera, you have to get up soon now because God only knows when we'll be able to come back again.'

Guys, yes I want to show you around, I really would love to! I wish I could say that out loud to them.

I was actually very happy to see all of them. It was a blessing that I made such nice and beautiful friends everywhere I went. I have always been blessed when it comes to friendship. I was always surrounded by good people, good friendships and good hearts. I really wanted to tell them that I was lucky to have them.

But where was Aryan? I couldn't see him. I wanted to ask Ruchi, because she knew about him. Had he contacted her? Why wasn't he here? Had he left me like this? I wanted the answers to all my questions. But for now, I was content to have all these people from my other home.

'Let's get you all some dinner,' my mother said to my friends, all of whom were probably jet-lagged and tired. 'Yea sure— Reena, I would love to eat something. But tell me, is it okay if we sit and eat here?' Lance asked my mother in a soft voice.

It was sweet how he called my mother by her first name. She was normally used to being called 'aunty'. I sensed my mother's amusement.

'Sure, dear. Why not?' she said and went out towards the kitchen to get things sorted for dinner.

'Aveera, we all are going to be here for two weeks—just get up really quick okay?' Lance said, looking straight into my eyes.

Lance, I can see you. Stop staring, I wanted to say. He was literally so close to my face, staring right into my eyes. I wanted to slap him playfully.

Meanwhile, my mother served everyone. There were two tables in my room, which they moved together to form a dining table of sorts. Meanwhile, the nurse came in with some food for me as well—in the form of some weird injection. I couldn't feel a thing when she injected it, which probably was a good thing.

'Such interesting food you're having, Aveera,' Lance couldn't help but joke. I wanted to snap at him—eat what they were eating. I was so glad they all were there, but somewhere my heart sank. Why wasn't Aryan around? I wanted to ask them about him but I just couldn't speak, I couldn't feel the power to lift up my hand and even make a gesture. While they all were enjoying their meal and randomly smiling at me, I kept thinking about how grateful I was to them. They had left no stone unturned to make me feel happy during this time. I still had my questions though: how I had ended up here and what all had gone down, but that was for when I'd get up. Suddenly, I started feeling out of breath. I could hear the beeping machine sounds.

'Oh god, what's happening? Guys!' Lance rushed towards me and everything suddenly became very hazy. It was only after I opened my eyes and could see what was happening that I realized I was feeling this crazy ache in my heart. It felt real. It was mind-numbingly painful.

'How are you, Aveera?' my mother asked and immediately continued, 'Enough now, you have to get up. It's time. You scared me so much…' she couldn't complete her sentence and broke down. I, on the other hand, was so blank. I barely realized that she was crying.

'She has been constantly thinking about something; there is some stress. We really need to get rid of that for her to recover quickly,' the doctor explained to my mom. I think I must have passed out for a long time. Everything around me seemed different from when I had last noticed them.

'Okay, doctor. We will do whatever is required. She passed out for seven days! This is scary. You need to tell me how long it's going to take for her to recover,' asked my crying mother. I was shocked to hear that I had passed out for a week! I had missed out on chilling with my friends and showing them around. They'd be gone so soon.

'Ma'am, as I keep telling you, it's difficult to say. She can hop up from her bed and be normal tomorrow, but it differs from patient to patient. She has been showing good signs of feeling and hearing things, which means she should be okay soon. As I have said, stay positive in front of her, please,' he said and went outside to talk to her in private. He gestured for her to join him there. They both discussed something, probably something about my health.

'Okay,' I heard my mother say, discomfort in her voice. I felt terrible that I had given her so much trouble. I heard Lance enter.

'Aveera, how are you honey?'

I am okay, I want to sit and talk to you all, I wanted to say. He placed his hand on my forehead. 'May Jesus bless you and may you recover soon,' he said, and it felt ethereal, as if he had just created something magical.

He smiled and said, 'You're going to be fine soon.'

The others came by and gave me a smile. They were finally going to go out that day to explore some of Punjab. They'd just been at home, looking after me, hoping I would open my eyes, but now that I was able to observe things again, my mother suggested they go out and explore the city a bit. She had arranged a driver for them so that they could easily commute.

I was excited for them.

But my heart felt quite hollow and I didn't know why—it was probably because of Aryan. I longed to see him. I didn't know where he was, or how he was doing. I wish I had made him meet my friends properly—then he would have known to contact them and come here. But there was no point thinking about it now. The heaviness felt real; it was more than a feeling— it was a physical pain I could strangely feel.

'Aveera, we'll see you later babe. Get well real soon now,' Ruchi said, and gave me a flying kiss. Ally and Andrew blew another in unison. Rishika was going with them to give them a tour of the city. She had been taking too many leaves from work just for me. How had I gotten so lucky to have found such friends?

Days passed, and my friends kept sightseeing and returning home early to check on me, hope still alive in their hearts. There was no sign of recovery. Everyone was impatient and more sorrowful as the days passed. They had all come all this way to see me, hoping that I would get better, but the journey ahead of me seemed rather long, filled with many more obstacles. The day before they were to leave, all I wanted to do was to get up and hug them and cry my heart out.

I feel the pain. I want to cry. I can feel emotions. Nurse! Please…please…help me get out of this! I wanted to scream. I wished I could get up and hug my friends and tell them how much I loved them. I wanted to get up and ask them about Aryan—my love, my life. Where was he? I wanted to cry.

That night, I lay awake, staring at the fan. The entire night passed. I thought of nothing but getting better.

'Good morning, Aveera, we're leaving in an hour. I want to tell you that you will indeed get better. We will come back again and we will meet you then. We'll go out, we'll party and we'll do your crazy dance too,' Andrew said with tears in his eyes. I could see everyone was emotional about this parting.

'I love you guys,' I said.

Wait! I said that out loud.

I had spoken, as loud as it had been in my head, and they had heard it!

'What? Aveera? Oh my god,' Lance said, scared and happy. Everyone else came hopping into the room, still struck by disbelief. I started crying and everyone came in and hugged me as I lay on the bed. My tears were real.

My mother called the doctor immediately. I could cry and I could talk. What was this sudden act of magic? I don't know what had just happened but I could feel everything—all the warmth, their touch, my tears, the pain. After this long and tiring journey, I could talk and I could say 'I love you' to them. It was priceless.

The doctor came in no time, and while everyone was waiting with all their excitement in check, he looked over my vitals, shining lights into my eyes.

'She's fine. She's out of the coma, and she can feel things. Just take it easy, Aveera. Don't stress about anything, okay?' he told everyone this, and then looked at me seriously, but with a smile.

'Thank you, thank you doctor,' my mother said; she had already called my father and he was on his way to meet his daughter—alive and well.

'Damn, girl! This is the best parting gift you could have given us,' Ally said with yet another hug.

'You guys are leaving?' I said slowly, I could speak but I had very little energy to express everything I felt.

'We have our flight to catch, baby. But we will be back soon. You recover until then and maybe you can come back to Scotland again?' she asked, excited but hesitant.

'Yeah honey. We missed you so much. Come back soon and then we're going to party!' Lance said and kissed my forehead.

'Yes!' I agreed, and they all smiled. I laughed weakly. They were just about to leave when I finally asked, 'Hey, Ruchi. Where is Aryan?'

'Aryan?' she asked, surprised.

'Yeah, the guy I was seeing. Remember you saw him once and smiled at us dancing?' I said, a little surprised myself. I remember her clearly giving me that look—a look of teasing your friend.

'Umm…Aveera, I don't remember any such incident,' she said.

'What, how is that possible?' I asked, even more surprised and confused now.

'Guys, Aryan was doing a PhD in the same school.' I said.

'Aveera, do you have his number?' Lance asked, trying his best to help.

'Number?' I was shocked. I spoke slowly. 'No, I never realized it, but I don't have his number. He was just around most of the time,' I said.

'Aveera, I know you told me about a guy, but we never met him. I will look for him on campus, and pull out the records for you,' Andrew said calmly. He seemed to know what to say. But this was all very confusing. None of my friends knew Aryan. Ruchi, who had clearly seen me with Aryan, remembered nothing about him! I couldn't believe what was happening.

I felt this sharp pain, and at the same time, everything became hazy and uncomfortable. Where was Aryan? Ruchi didn't remember him. What was all this?

'Aveera, we've got to leave right now, but we will call and tell you about Aryan. Okay?' said Andrew, trying his best to comfort me.

'Okay,' I replied with a sigh. *This was not normal.*

I bid them all goodbye, and let them hug me real tight. I was still not able to move my arms or grasp anything. I was sad that they all had to leave. I hadn't been able to spend any time with them at all.

But what was more painful was that Aryan was nowhere to be seen. I didn't know what to do. I didn't have his number! As I waved goodbye to my friends, something seemed to switch off in my life. Something that didn't feel right. I was in a state of shock and confusion. What was really happening? Nothing made sense.

'Maa, you remember?' I asked as she closed the door and returned to sit by my bed, 'I told you about a guy I was falling for?' I asked my mother in a rather rushed tone.

'Yes, Aveera. Calm down first. I remember you told me— while we were Facetiming. But you never sent me his pictures or even told me his name,' she said, gesturing with her hands.

'Oh,' I said. *Why had I forgotten to send her a picture?* 'I guess…I forgot,' I said finally, quiet and sad.

'Don't stress too much. You say you love him. And he loved you, right? Just be patient. Your friends are going to talk to him once they reach there. But it's strange that you don't have his number,' she said, confused herself.

'Just go to bed. You need some sleep, and lots of water. Do not stress now, Aveera,' she said.

'Yes,' I said. Clearly I was not 'not stressing'. This was too much for me considering how beautiful a time I shared with

Aryan back in Scotland. And suddenly, I had no news of him. It was bizarre how things had changed so much.

'Aveera, go to bed. I can see you're still thinking,' said my mother.

'Yeah, Mom,' I said, and as I was about to close my eyes, my dad knocked on the door. I smiled at him as he came in.

'My bacha, thank god, you've come back to us,' he said, teary-eyed.

'I love you, dad,' I said and hugged him. I was still weak. I had eaten nothing solid for the longest time. 'Take care, take rest. Your mother told me you've been thinking ever since you woke up. Don't do that bete. Give it time. You'll have all of your answers. I know you don't remember a lot of things—your friends and we will tell you everything, but for now, you need to take rest,' he said, brushing a hand through my hair just like he would when I was a child.

'Yes, I guess I should sleep. I am feeling tired anyway,' I said, and turned around and closed my eyes, hoping I would not dream or think too much.

That day, I actually slept well. I must have been tired, despite how worried I was. But when I woke up, there was this sudden hollowness, the same kind that I had felt a few days earlier. It seemed as if the world wasn't real and it was all a dream. I stepped out of the bed slowly, and wore my slippers and went straight to the washroom. I don't know what happened, I started to cry. It was bad, very bad. I looked at myself in the mirror and cried and kept questioning myself: why was I crying? I was out of a coma, my friends had been so kind, my mom and dad were with me, everything was getting back to normal, but still, I was inconsolable and I had no idea why.

'Aveera, you all right?' It was my brother calling to me.

'Yea, bro. I am okay, just coming,' I said, wiping my tears.

It's okay. It's okay, you are fine. It'll all be fine, I told myself and took deep breaths. I washed my face and went out. I seemed to have the energy for a normal day.

'Were you crying?' he asked at the door.

'No…' as I said that, I broke down again.

'Oye oye, Aveera, Don't cry…what's wrong? Tell me.'

'I don't know, I just don't know. Can I tell you about someone?' I asked him.

'Anything. Tell me, what is it?' he asked and took me back to my bed. My parents weren't at home. They had gone to offer prayers at the temple for my well-being. I heaved a sigh of relief; I didn't want them to see me like this.

'There is this guy…Aryan…' I began as he listened. He looked intent, and concerned.

'I love him, bro. I really do. We spent a really good time in Scotland, and we definitely wanted to get married. I had returned from Iceland, and he was there at the airport to surprise me with a ring. When I got out of the car near my school…well…he wasn't there. I do not remember anything after that. I know a car rammed into me but after that, the only memory I have is of waking up at home and seeing you all. But I don't know where Aryan is.' I said, tears still falling from my eyes.

'Hey, hey. Slow down and stop crying first,' he said. I didn't realize how hard I was crying, breathlessly, without even pausing for a second.

I sighed while still crying. 'So you are saying that you never even gave him your number or took his number?' he asked after I had explained why I was so confused.

'No. I don't understand why. We just kept meeting; I know

it sounds bizarre, but that's how it was,' I said, not understanding it all myself.

'This is weird, Aveera. But you need to relax. You've just recovered. As you said, your friends are going to look for him. Right? I am sure he must also be looking for you,' he said, trying his best to comfort me.

'Yeah, that's true. I hope I hear back from Ruchi soon. What time are they landing, again?' I asked.

'They've just landed. I got a text,' he said.

'Oh. Okay. I'll check with them,' I said, wiping my tears.

'Listen, we all love you. Everything will get be back to normal,' he said.

I hugged him. We were quiet for a minute, trying our best to feel the truth in those words, to finally feel at home.

A week passed by and I had regained some of my energy, but not all of it. I had begun to eat full meals in between meeting relatives and sleeping. The medicines continued. I hadn't heard anything from my friends about Aryan, even though they checked in every day. But then, one morning, I received a call from Andrew in the middle of the day. I picked up, excited to hear whatever he would have to say.

'Aveera, I checked. There's no guy named Aryan in the entire PhD course,' Andrew said, surprised himself, without missing a beat.

'What?' I stood shell-shocked, trying to reason with myself. 'How is this possible? I saw his ID, it said Aryan.' I explained in panic.

'Aveera, I checked the entire system; there's no one named Aryan. Trust me,' he said.

'Oh God. Andrew—Andrew, how is it even possible? Listen, please…please pull some strings and get some CCTV footage from near the hostel garden…from November. I was with him. Please Andrew. I beg of you,' I broke down while saying this.

'Hey, calm down. I will do something. Just don't cry. I will get back to you; give me some time. I'll definitely do something,' he said and hurriedly cut the call. I immediately dialled Ruchi's number.

'Ruchi, Ruchi listen, please. Andrew called me to tell me that there is no one named Aryan in our school. Ruchi, how is this possible? You saw me with him. Please just try to remember and do something. Please, Ruchi,' I said, crying out loud.

'Aveera. Please stop crying. *Main karti hoon kuch* (I'll do something). I swear, I don't remember seeing you with any guy anywhere, least of all the pub in Paris. But I will talk to Andrew, and we will make sure we find out about him as soon as possible,' she said.

'Ruchi, we saw each other in Paris. I met him throughout our time there,' I said, wiping away my tears.

'What?' she said, absolutely shocked. 'Wow, I had no idea, Aveera. Is that why you kept going off on your own?' she asked.

'Yeah, because he wasn't ready to meet you guys. Neither was I ready to make that happen. But please, help me with this.' I was now worried about where he was, and even about who he was. I had no idea what was going on.

Meanwhile, my brother was right by my side. I told him not to talk to my parents about this. I didn't want to worry them any more. 'Don't worry, I won't talk to them, but you have to calm down and stop crying. Your health should be your focus now. You need to feel energetic, but if you keep crying, that's not going to happen, Aveera,' he said kindly.

'Yeah,' I said, trying my best to agree with what he was saying.

Nine

Days went by and there was no sign of Aryan; no one told me anything. My friends from Delhi came to visit again. And Rishika was there too. Kabir and the others were constantly checking in on me.

'Aveera, please stop thinking so much about him,' Kabir said, meaning well.

'How can I not think about it, Kabir? How?' I asked him, angry.

All my conversations with them were the same. My parents began to worry about me. I was eating and walking well, but I always seemed to be caught up in thought—they saw me pacing to and fro often.

After a few days, I received a call from Andrew. 'Aveera, hi…ummm…can we talk, darling?' he asked. Something about his tone was odd. I was scared.

'Yeah, Andrew, please tell me. Please,' I said, still hoping that he would say something positive.

'I pulled some strings, as you asked, and got CCTV footage. I saw you…I did see you, but…' he was quiet and hesitant.

'And what, Andrew?' I asked, impatient. I wanted to know about Aryan.

'There was no one with you, Aveera. You were talking to yourself. You held your own hand and were walking by yourself.

There was no one there,' he finally said. It felt like the entire world had crashed down on me. I didn't want to believe him.

'What? What are you saying? What are you even saying, Andrew? No, this cannot be true. How is it even possible?' I asked, numb, trying my best to reason calmly.

'Aveera, Aveera. You need to calm down. Please. There was no one in the footage, Aveera,' he said, trying his best to make sure I wasn't breaking apart.

'I'll talk later,' I said and quickly cut the call before he could say anything. I couldn't talk. I was running out of breath.

'Tej!' I called out for my brother, and when he came running, I asked for a glass of water. He came back immediately and held the glass to my lips, helping me drink from it slowly.

'You okay, Aveera?' he asked.

'Yeah, I just need to be alone,' I said. He looked worried but he left, closing the door behind him.

Everything seemed confusing and all too strange. What was happening? There is 'no Aryan'? It didn't make sense. I did everything possible to try and find out about him—scanned records on my phone, looked through my receipts, even checked Facebook and Instagram again. But there was no trace of a person named Aryan who matched the handsome man I remembered.

I started to feel more and more exhausted as the days went by. One night, I suddenly woke up and found that I was drenched in my own sweat. I had no memory of what had happened in my dream. I couldn't breathe properly and was panicking—the entire world was going somewhere and I had been left behind. I gulped down some water and turned the fan on full speed.

It's okay, it's okay. I told myself and tried to relax. Still scared, I went back to bed. The next morning, I woke up with a heavy feeling and tears in my eyes, as if I had been crying all night. I didn't want to get out of bed. I lay there for the longest time. I finally moved the blanket away and brushed my teeth, only to feel tired again. I went back to bed.

'Aveera, breakfast, bacha?' my mother asked, knocking at my door.

'I'll have it in here,' I said, asking her to serve me with a weak smile.

'Okay,' she said and asked our house help to serve breakfast in bed. He came and served me the food. I took one bite and let it fall back on the plate. Hours passed and I still wasn't hungry. Eating food seemed like a task. A constant heaviness occupied me and my mind felt like it had been numbed. Everything seemed vague...and fake. Nothing made sense at all.

Days passed and the numbness only increased. I barely spoke with my friends who came to visit, staying silent when they called. I wouldn't talk to anyone. It was almost like I wanted to be lonely. And I was constantly angry and frustrated, so much so that I fought and argued with my parents a lot. They were obviously worried.

They had so many questions: 'What happened, beta? Why is your mood off?' my mother asked one evening.

'Nothing. Why are you always troubling me? Just leave me alone,' I replied, turning away at the dinner table.

'This is not how you talk to your mother, Aveera. What has happened to you?' my dad asked sternly.

'Sorry, okay?' I said and rushed inside my room.

Each day passed the same way. I stopped turning on the lights and stayed in a dark room. From appreciating beauty and socializing daily, I became lonely and sad. The panic attacks continued every other day. I woke up crying almost daily and I never slept peacefully.

I was sinking. The heartache and the pressure of not having any answers, of remembering wrong… I just wanted it to stop. *Shut up. Shut up. Shut up!* I slapped at the sides of my head, wanting to stop thinking. I was always crying.

Please, God. Please. Help me. Stop this, please…

I broke down. I didn't know I could cry so much. Each day I just wanted to vent. It wasn't right. I spoke with my friends once in a while but I was in bed most of the time. The painkillers I took for my recurring headaches weren't much help and neither were my parents' attempts, as kind as they were. I tried to put on a brave face in front of them.

'Aveera, it's been over three months now. Now that you do not want to go to Scotland, come help me in the business. It will be a change for you,' my dad said.

I liked this idea. Even though I felt broken, like I was almost dead and had no energy, I decided that I would go to work with my dad. My friends had already started with the job-hunting process, while Ruchi had already gotten herself an interview. I was struggling with my identity crisis. I couldn't write anything and I was lonely. I hadn't heard from Aryan and none of my friends could trace him. I had no job. I felt like a loser. Kabir had stopped talking to me; I was always whining and it's true, people can tolerate only so much. It felt bad though. Things seemed messed up, so going out and working with my dad seemed like a good idea and I smiled after a long time.

'Yeah, Dad. I'm on board! I'll come with you from tomorrow and let's see where I can work,' I said and he smiled at me. The next morning, I woke up with the same numbness, but it was a little better, I was excited too.

I got up, got ready and put on a brave face and went to work. I met so many people. My dad introduced me to the core team and explained the operational work that I was going to handle. It didn't seem difficult. I understood everything he tried to explain and decided to get busy. I wanted to keep myself distracted.

'All right, I'll leave you to it then,' my dad said and went into his office. Slowly and gradually, I mingled with the staff. They were quite nice and I started to understand the kind of work I was supposed to do as the days passed.

I engrossed myself in papers and books. For a change, I was actually thinking about something else and it felt nice.

'How's it going, Aveera?' dad asked a few days later.

'Good, Dad. It's nice,' I replied.

'Great, bacha, keep going. I told you, you just needed a change. There was nothing wrong with you,' he said.

'You were right,' I said, convincing myself as well.

Maybe there was nothing wrong with me. Maybe I just thought too much. It was just a phase. Maybe it was just nothing.

I engaged myself with work after that. Day by day, I got better at it, and I even laughed during the day with my colleagues. My father was mostly out for business meetings.

'You're such a happy soul, Aveera,' one of my colleagues at work said one afternoon.

'Yeah?' I asked, thanking her for thinking that way.

'Yeah dude. You're awesome!' another agreed.

'Haha, not really,' I said, and changed the topic, returning to the work at hand.

For a brief while, I thought that it was all getting better and working out well. But the moment I would step back into my house, I just wanted to go to bed all the time. I wanted to breathe. There was so much I felt that I kept hidden, that just wanted to get out. All these conversations that I had, all the things my colleagues used to talk about, didn't make any difference. I still felt the same. I still felt lonely.

Sometimes, in the office, I would hear people laughing and talking. I would laugh with them. But I didn't feel a thing. I didn't find things funny enough to even laugh or smile.

I started to lose all the confidence, all the faith I had once had. I didn't know what was right and what was wrong. I started to doubt myself. My friends were excelling in their lives and I was happy, really happy for them. But I felt as if I didn't deserve a thing, as if I wasn't made to excel. I just felt useless.

Please stop thinking, I beg you, please, I told myself while sitting on my bathroom floor, one evening. I had soaked my shirt with my tears and my eyes were swollen.

A hammering pain had started in my head. I wanted to smash my head into the wall if that would make it stop buzzing constantly.

I screamed and I broke down, holding my face in my hands. I fell on the bathroom floor and cried for hours on the cold tiles. I had no idea what was really happening to me. All I knew was that my body and mind hurt when it wasn't numb. I was hollow.

What should I do? I talked to myself as I lay on the bathroom floor. I got up and looked at myself in the mirror. 'Aveera, what is wrong with you? Don't cry please,' I said out loud to myself and again started to cry. My eyes were so swollen all the time. All I could do was talk to myself. Some of my friends had given up on me, but some of them were really trying to talk to me. Kabir called the next afternoon, on a weekend. I didn't want to listen to him.

'Kabir, listen, just go away, all right? I do not want to talk. And stop saying, "I love you" all the time, okay? I don't love you. Just leave me alone. I am doing just fine,' I snapped at him as I picked up the call.

'Listen, please, Aveera. What is making you so upset?' he asked.

'Why the hell can't you back off? I just need some space, please,' I said and cut the call and broke down. I didn't want to do this to him, but I had no idea why I was being such a bad friend.

'I am bad, I am so bad,' I said out loud as I went back inside the bathroom to wash my swollen face.

'You're mean and selfish, Aveera. You're not a good friend, not a good daughter, nothing,' I told myself in the mirror. I was scared, scared of being left alone and of being away from everyone. Aryan wasn't there in my life any more, I had no idea about him at all, I was losing all my friends. Rishika still came to check in on me. My friends from Scotland—Ruchi, Ally, Lance and Andrew were constantly checking in on me but my heart just wasn't in any of these friendships. I wasn't happy about anything, I had no mental peace. Imagine being in a situation where you cannot feel the silence for even a second, everything around you is buzzing and humming and making noise—wouldn't you be tired? I was in that zone. Even sitting in my room alone, I felt like I was always around millions of people and trillions of thoughts.

'I am going out; I'll be late,' I told my mom that evening.

'But where are you going, Aveera?' she asked.

'Out!' I told her, closing the door before she could ask more questions. I drove to a pub nearby. I had a couple of drinks. I hoped that it would soothe my mind. I had found some solace in alcohol, but sometimes it didn't work, and it would make me want to cry even harder. Like there were thousands of emotions in my heart that wanted to come out and breathe.

'Hey, you alone here?' a group of random strangers sidled up to me.

'Yeah, sure. Me and my countless thoughts. Want to chill?' I asked them.

'Haha, sure,' they said and started to drag me to dance with them. And I did. I danced for a while, lost in the music, and then I started to fool around. But thanks to my senses, I took off immediately. I felt a lump in my throat. I puked outside and drove back home in a very drunken state. I had my keys, so fortunately I didn't have to ask my parents to open the door for me. Troubling them was the last thing I wanted.

I went to bed and just stared at the wall for the longest time, wondering what was wrong with me. I decided I would stop. I would just start being happy. I would just start to think more positively. This was it, this was the inner calling and I wanted to act on it.

The next morning, I was back at work. I was getting work done. I cracked some jokes, laughed with my colleagues and chilled with them after work ended. It was a good day. I left for home on a positive note. I chatted with my mom for a bit so she could see me this way. As I went into my room, I couldn't hold the emotions I had kept inside the entire day. I pulled up my comforter and rolled it over me and screamed loudly, but I had covered my mouth with a pillow so I wouldn't be heard.

You were happy and you were smiling; why the hell are you crying Aveera? What is wrong with you? You need to stop.

I started to cry even more after I had tried to give myself a pep talk. I slapped myself a few times. This was the hardest part of the day. Trying to control myself even though I didn't know what I was controlling me. Everyone around me at work thought of me as someone with a lot of cheer, who spread happiness, but deep down, I was fighting my own battle—a battle I felt I wasn't capable of fighting any more.

This kept on for days and days. I had become very weak, my eyes were swollen all the time. When I would go to bed, I prayed for the same thing, 'God, I wish to not open my eyes tomorrow, please.' But the morning would come, and I hated having to open my eyes. I didn't want to wake up. In spite of having everyone around me, and all the necessities in life, I was alone. It felt as if I was under water, an inch deeper, every day. It felt as if I could breathe, and then, soon enough it would get very tedious to breathe or even see anything clearly. The urge to breathe was declining with each passing day. It felt like an extremely tedious task.

My rage had only grown. It seemed to me that I had multiple personalities jostling for space, each expressing itself on a whim. Most of the time, I just wanted to break something. I had this strong urge to punch someone or something and I often punched the wall, as hard as I could, to harm myself. I was getting weaker. Self-destruction and any kind of physical pain helped distract me. It made it easier to deal with what I was going through. This continued and I felt like I had pulled myself away from everyone who had once been close to me. I hurt the people I loved so much, and every time I did, my self-doubt and guilt would increase. I hated myself. I hated everything around me. I wasn't doing well professionally and I wasn't doing any good in my personal life. I didn't have a reason to be happy.

One day, there was no one at home except for the house help. I had a day off from work and I was in a very gloomy mood. I had started to hate the light. More than four months had passed, and I was depressed. I was lonely. I was empty.

I had put on some dim lights in my room, the only lights I would leave on, even in the mornings.

The day wasn't any different from the rest. I was just lying on my bed, wide awake in the morning, without any sunlight. I don't know what came over me, but I suddenly took the stairs and went upstairs to the roof. 'You could have been better, Aveera,' I told myself and stood right at the edge, leaning against the rails. I had finally decided. I would end my life.

'You don't deserve any happiness, this is it—,' and as I was finishing my sentence, I heard footsteps approach.

'What the hell, Aveera?' Rishika pulled me by my arm towards her. She had a dangerous expression on her face.

'Rishika—'

'What were you trying to do?' she asked, dragging me aside.

'Nothing…I…' I broke down before I could finish the sentence and I hugged her.

'Aveera, what is happening? Talk to me. Don't suffer in silence,' she said. 'Let's go down. Come,' she said and took me downstairs by the hand. I was still in tears.

We went into my room.

'Sit. Now tell me, what is going on, Aveera?' she asked, handing a glass of water to me.

'Rishika…I miss you,' I said in between loud sobs.

'Listen, I am here with you. Everyone is with you, but please, tell me what's going on in your head. Just let it all out,' she begged.

'I feel lonely, I feel stuck, I feel worthless and useless. My friends have stopped talking to me. Some of them are trying too hard to help me out but I just can't seem to find peace. I feel like I am dying each day, and I just don't want to wake up. I am happy at one point in time and then, soon enough,

I just can't seem to make sense of anything and I just want everything around me to stop. My mind is never quiet and I am constantly thinking about one thing or the other. I keep talking to myself to calm myself down, but Rishika, it doesn't work for even a second. It has become so hard to sleep at night. I haven't slept peacefully for the longest time. I wake up in the middle of the night drenched in sweat, afraid, and I don't sleep after that. I cannot trouble my parents, they've always been so nice to me. What a disgrace I have become to them. I just cry all the time, Rishika. I am scared, I am very scared, I think I'm depressed. I need help Rishika,' I said and just cried my heart out through this monologue.

'Whoa, slow down and stop crying, first of all,' she said and continued. 'Aveera, you *are* depressed. It's okay to feel low in life. That does not make you a disgrace. You are a beautiful person, my love. You bring happiness into the lives of people, so stop giving too much importance to the negative thoughts that seem to plague you. Let's consult a therapist. There is nothing to feel ashamed about. We will go to the best one and have your sessions booked immediately,' she said and started to thumb through her phone.

'But, Rishika—' Before I could finish, Rishika said, 'No buts and no ifs; let me do this now. I am in this with you. We all are, all right?'

'Yeah,' I said, a little relieved. I guess I needed help after all. It might help to go see an absolute outsider, have them listen to me and help me gain my confidence back.

Rishika made a few calls and finalized an appointment with Dr Karan, a renowned therapist/psychologist. 'You have your first appointment tomorrow, Aveera. You'll be out of it soon, I promise. Just trust him and let yourself be free—let all your thoughts out,' she said.

'Thank you Rishika. Thanks a lot,' I said and hugged her.

I think she stood and hugged me for the longest time, I couldn't have asked for anything else. She was not annoyed. She had been encouraging me every single day, had been kind to me all this while, had never given up on me.

Next morning, I got ready for my first session with my therapist, Dr Karan. I was quite scared and intimidated. I had never been to a psychologist before.

Ten

I knocked at his open door. 'Hi, Dr Karan,' I greeted him. 'Aveera, come, please,' he said, pulling out a chair for me.

'Thank you, Doctor,' I said and sat down, as comfortably as I could.

'Water, tea or coffee?' he asked with a smile.

'Water would be okay,' I said and took the glass of water he offered me. I was nervous, so I gulped it down in one go.

'Aveera, why are you nervous? Slow down. Don't drink water that fast,' he said.

'Sorry about that. This is my first time,' I said.

'First time? Hahaha. It's not a big deal, Aveera. Someone is just here to listen to everything you say, that's all. When I say everything—it means anything you have possibly ever thought about,' he said. 'Visiting a therapist is something of a taboo in our society, and is regarded as a huge deal, but it's not. There's no first time or anything. I am just here to listen, so do not worry.'

'Yeah,' I said and smiled.

'So, tell me your story, Aveera.'

'Story?' I asked, surprised.

'Yes, just tell me everything about your life. What made you come to me?'

'Oh, where should I begin?'

'From the beginning. How you feel at the moment, what is going on in your life—everything.'

'All right,' I sighed and took a deep breath. It was time to let everything out.

'I feel very exhausted, worn out and tired. I feel like I have no energy or oxygen left in me and I am just trying really hard to breathe all the time. I have disappointed a lot of my friends; they have been trying to help me, to talk to me...but I just get angry, you know. Sometimes I feel like what they say is nonsense. There's nothing that makes sense in what they say. I have so many expectations from them, and I am sure they have the same from me...but it seems like I end up disappointing them. My family has been so tense because of me all this while. I just don't know what to do,' I said in a rush.

'Here, have some water. Vent.'

'This is what I have been doing all this while. Venting. My mind doesn't shut up. It keeps talking. I haven't been able to sleep for the longest time and it just annoys me and makes me tired. So I want to hurt myself and cause myself pain...it kind of makes me feel better,' I explained, a little ashamed.

'Aveera, I want you to stop right there,' he interrupted. 'Why do you feel the need to harm yourself?'

'Because it distracts me from the mental pain and thoughts for a while.'

'So you harm yourself?'

'Yeah,' I said, disappointed in myself.

'Aveera, self-harm will only cause self-doubt. You'll look at the scars and remind yourself of your weaknesses. It will make you repeat the same patterns. Have you ever thought of channelling that anger somewhere else? Not harming yourself?' he asked.

'Like where?' I asked, not very interested in his advice.

'Maybe a run? You know what, let's try this for a while. I want you to get up in the morning and go for a fifteen-minute run. After which, you will note down how you felt, what you were thinking while you were running, and how you felt later in the day. Okay?' he said.

'Homework, seriously?' I asked with a laugh.

'Yes, seriously. Now this is the end of the session for today,' he said.

'Oh,' I said, surprised that time had passed so quickly. 'Okay, I will see you soon,' I said.

'Yeah, and Aveera?' he called me as I was leaving.

'Yes, Doctor?'

'Don't forget to drink plenty of water. It helps to de-stress,' he said.

'Okay,' I said.

What a weird doctor. How can water help me de-stress? I didn't even know if I wanted to come back and see him. But it felt like it was my only chance at getting better, so I wanted to at least try.

I returned for the next session a little more comfortable and began to speak as soon as I sat down. Dr Karan already had a glass of water ready for me.

'So I was very happy about getting into my dream school in Scotland. Everything was perfect. I have always been close to my friends and it was a little hard to leave them and go for a year in Scotland. But it was also very exciting at the same time. Going abroad and living a different life, meeting new people—it was nice,' I said, looking up at the ceiling, thinking about happier times.

'Carry on, Aveera. You were happy. I see you are smiling;

tell me more about it,' he said.

'So I reached Scotland, but throughout the journey, and even after—I kept encountering this strange guy named Aryan. It was always weird to just bump into him in the oddest of ways.'

'Oh, a strange guy? Why was he strange?' he asked inquisitively.

'I mean, he was always at the most random of places. I went to meet my friends in Delhi and while returning on the train, he was sitting right next to me. He knew almost everything about me. I was creeped out; I had no idea who he was. I again met him on the plane while travelling to Scotland. He just kept popping up in my life—one way or the other. I tried to find him on social media but I couldn't,' I said. The memory of not being able to locate him was still fresh and it saddened me.

'I see some sadness in your eyes right now. Why, Aveera?'

'Oh, hmm…nothing actually.'

I didn't want to talk about Aryan. It just made me feel upset thinking about the fact that he hadn't paid any heed to calling me or checking up on me. This was the hardest part of going down memory lane. It'd only bring me pain and anger.

'Okay, so there's something about this guy,' he said, nodding his head as if he were worried about it.

'Hmm, yeah. I guess so.'

'Go on, Aveera. Don't let your memories from the past chain you in shackles in the present.'

I looked towards him and continued, 'So when I went to Scotland, I found him there too. He was actually a student at the school I was in. He was pursuing a PhD in medicine,' I said.

'Oh, a doctor? I see. Must be very smart, haan?' he joked.

'Hmm.'

'All right, Aveera, go on. Don't feel bad about the good

things you experienced in the past. Remember them with a smile. They were good then. Something good will come later too,' he said when I stopped speaking.

'Yeah, so we started meeting often…and it was just…very nice. It was going great. I started to fall for that weird guy, and soon, we realized that we both loved each other. It was the kind of love you imagine in a fairytale, you know?' I said and continued, 'It was perfect. He was the kind of guy I have always thought of being with. Just like someone I'd ever imagine,' I said with a smile on my face remembering him and missing him at the same time.

'And then?'

'We eventually started dating. We both decided not to tell our friends because it was just our little secret. I just didn't want to share him with anyone and wanted him close to my heart. It was personal and I wanted it to stay that way.'

'Keep it close, *yes*. But did you ever feel like making him meet your friends and making him a part of their lives too?'

'No. I just didn't want anyone or anything to jinx it. It was so real and warm that I was afraid.'

'Right, okay.'

'So we continued with our relationship in our own dreamy world. We travelled, had fun. I was at a very happy place in my life. I made good friends, all of whom were loving and supportive and it was the best kind of things and places I could have asked for. I was in Iceland with my friends. You know, Andrew proposed to Lance, there. They're the cutest couple ever,' I said with a smile on my face and took a long pause. Dr Karan was looking towards me, raising one eyebrow.

'And?' he finally broke the silence.

'And you know, when I reached the airport, Aryan came

to pick me up at the airport and guess what?' I asked, with a gleam and hope in my eyes.

'What?'

'He proposed to me,' I said with a smile.

'Oh wow.'

'Yeah, we were in love and everything fit just right,' I said.

I continued after a moment, trying my best to lighten the mood. 'Anyway, we shared a cab back to school. And soon, I met with an accident and landed up comatose in India,' I laughed. 'Here I am.'

Dr Karan wasn't amused.

'Right. So you were in a coma and after you recovered, you're here… Aveera, tell me, what happened between the time when you got out of the coma and now?' he asked, as if he had the solution to everything.

'Well, when I gained my senses, I was in India. My friends from Scotland had come to visit me, everyone was there, all my friends from college too…but Aryan wasn't. He was nowhere to be seen. It's just bizarre how we were about to be married, and now…there's no news of him,' I said with a very worried tone.

'Hmmm. Did you try calling him, or you know, ask your friends to talk to him?'

'Yeah, about that, we never really exchanged numbers. Somehow, we just planned and met, almost always,' I explained. 'Ever since then, things have been off-track. It was sudden. I now cry a lot. I smile and laugh superficially, but I am actually dying inside. I am insecure about Aryan. Why'd he leave me? And my career is falling apart. All my friends are doing well, and here I am, just sitting like a useless person—no goals or ambitions in life and—'

'Your friends are doing well, how so?' he interrupted to

question me. Then seeing my confusion, he continued, 'Aveera, if everyone around you—and that includes you—are doing things at the same place and the same time, then how can anything be different?' he asked and continued. 'Imagine all the flowers wishing to bloom in the same season. Imagine summer existing in winter. Everything cannot happen at the same time, Aveera. People come with their own clocks. Some taste success early in life and some experience more and then taste that success.'

I sighed.

'Winters will come when it is time for winter and summers arrive when it is time for summer. All the flowers have a different time to bloom. The day goes by and the night comes as per their time. This is the way in which the universe has been working all this while, and it will keep going on like that,' he said. He was questioning the self-doubts I had, and it wasn't wrong. I had been in an accident. Things weren't easy for me to suddenly help me flourish.

'That makes sense,' I said.

'Yeah. Please continue. You were not able to contact Aryan; what else made you feel so weak, Aveera?' he asked.

Aren't you supposed to tell me? I thought, but I spoke anyway. 'I don't know; I just fail to understand how he could cut me off like that and what was really going on. And I don't know, I have felt this hollowness before Scotland as well. Aryan sort of...filled that for me. And it just aches to think about it,' I said, finally shedding the tears I was trying my best to control.

'Okay, you know how strong you are? You know why? Because you can feel all these emotions. Crying is not a sign of weakness, Aveera; it's a sign of bravery and strength. You have been super brave all this while. Here, have some water,' he said, passing me the glass of water.

'Thanks, Dr Karan,' I said. He was a kind man.

'Aveera, listen, I want you to go home today and pen down everything you remember with Aryan. All the good things… and the bad ones—each little experience you've had with him, the way it made you feel and everything that was happening around you when you were with him.'

'But why?' I asked, super confused about why he was giving me this kind of homework.

'Just do it. Trust me,' he said and smiled.

'Okay,' I agreed.

He somehow had a very calming personality and it made me feel comfortable around him. I could be myself. It might have been that because I didn't know him at all, I was able to talk about everything.

'That's it for today. You are very strong, trust me,' he said, and I smiled.

'I'll see you,' I said and left, wondering about Aryan.

That night, I spent two hours remembering every minute detail I had shared with Aryan, reliving all the memories we made. It was painful but very refreshing to pen it all down. It just made me feel as if there were things flowing when I thought of him. I kept that notebook close to me and went off to bed. I was looking forward to my next session with Dr Karan. It felt like I had a friend, a different kind of friend, but a friend all the same.

Meanwhile, I was being a little distant at home. I still had panic attacks but I wasn't afraid of them as much.

'Hi Aveera, how are you?' Dr Karan asked at the next session.

'I am good, Doc,' I said with a smile.

'So did you complete the task I gave you?

'Yes, here,' and I gave him my notebook.

'Okay, let's see all your memories with him,' he said and started to go through the notes I had made. In this short span, I had made a fairly large number of memories.

'Okay, Aveera, I need you to pay attention to me, okay?' he suddenly looked at me, closing the notebook. He had a serious expression.

'Now you say that you are not able to contact him, right? What about your friends? They can't find him anywhere? They never saw you with him?' he asked.

'No, in fact Andrew checked the CCTV footage of the area I met and chatted with him. I don't know why he says that there wasn't anyone in the footage, expect for me. It was just me talking to myself. How stupid would that be! I don't believe it,' I said, scoffing.

'Right,' he said and continued. I didn't know where he was going and I was scared.

'Aveera, do you realize all these things you've written are only from when you've wanted to create some memories? It happens when there's something you have always wanted?'

'What do you mean?' I asked, surprised by his line of thought.

'You met Aryan in the train, right after you left Delhi. You were feeling low, worried about how you'd feel lonely in Scotland. Your friend Kabir is quite close to you, right? You both share a love. You felt sad about leaving everyone, right?' he asked.

'Yeah, but how does that have anything to do with this?'

'Yeah, listen to me, Aveera. You then met Aryan in Scotland, always whenever something loving and nice was happening around you, whenever you wanted to feel secure—just like others,' he said and continued. 'You saw Andrew and Lance getting engaged, and then you wanted exactly that in your life.

So you went back and Aryan proposed to you. You were in Paris, the city of love—he was there, just the way you wanted him to be.'

'Yeah, that's what I told you,' I said, confused and baffled now.

'Aveera, Aryan is not real. He is just a figment of your imagination,' he said, taking a deep breath.

'What?' I said, feeling like everything had just slipped away from right under my feet. 'What are you saying?' My world seemed to crash. I looked around in a panic.

'Calm down, Aveera. Let me help you connect the dots,' he said kindly.

'What?' I said. I was still worried. My heart beat so fast that I thought I would have a heart attack.

'Aveera, sometimes, a person can start to want things so deeply that they feel that everything they imagine is real. But in reality, it isn't. Aryan has always been a figment of your imagination. You always wanted it to be true, and you made it true,' he said in a very calm tone.

'Doctor, what is happening? What does that mean? I'm sick and delusional?' I asked.

'No, you are fine and you will be fine. It is just that you must believe me. People start perceiving things in such a way that the things soon become a powerful fascination and their beliefs turn into reality. For you, the kind of guy Aryan was, you've always wanted someone like that. None of your friends ever saw him, you did not have his number, nothing. You went into a coma and your brain did not think of anything or see anything for a while, which is why you cannot find Aryan anywhere now,' he explained.

It was too much to take in. Too much information. I was

feeling restless and I didn't want to believe what he was saying.

'I need something to drink,' I said, feeling faint and lightheaded.

Dr Karan quickly got up and brought me a glass of glucose and water.

'Thank you, Doctor,' I said, drinking it slowly, ignoring all the feelings that his words had evoked.

'This is going to be all okay, all right? Don't put too much pressure thinking about it. You'll see for yourself that there wasn't anyone with you all this while. It was just you and yourself—and your imagination,' he said.

I didn't say much but I was lost in my own world, thinking about everything he had said. *What about everything I experienced?* I was confused.

'Tell me something, you said you felt hollow before moving to Scotland; why is that?' he asked.

'I don't know; I have always had a sadness looming over me. I felt that I have never accomplished anything in life,' I said, still not over the fact that Aryan was never really real.

'Did you date anyone in the past, Aveera?' he asked.

'Yeah, three or four guys. I won't really call them dating. They were a series of failed relationships; nothing worked out with any of them. All of them had problems with me,' I said truthfully.

'See, because you had so many failed relationships, you wanted someone to make you feel complete. The way you wanted. The desire for it was powerful and you started to imagine someone real. Why did it not work with any of them?' he asked after a brief pause, as he watched me fumble to be comfortable in my seat. I didn't know how to make sense of what he had said, what he kept repeating.

'I was too ambitious, you know. I was confused all the time. I was the cause of the problems every time. I was indecisive. I wanted love, I wanted someone to properly understand me. None of them could do that,' I said.

He nodded and I sighed. It was true, I had a very unsatisfying life when it came to dating. Also I was always confused about my career. I mostly lived in the past or the future, never really in the present. We sat there quietly for some time. I tried to figure out what had just happened. This revelation changed everything.

'You know, you missed out on a lot, Aveera. You always thought what it could have been like and what it should be like, but never about what it actually was,' he said finally. 'Your generation has too many preconceived notions about love and life. They have forgotten to just live. You have a set of ideas about love in your life that makes you forget to enjoy the moment. But you know what? You are a human being, that's how you learn. You make mistakes, you learn from them and then you grow. It doesn't stop there. You will keep making different mistakes. This is part of growing, this is part of life,' he said.

'Yeah, it's just that I can't believe all this. I was so alone, and so hollow, to be precise.'

'That will not stay; take it easy. I will meet you for your next session. For now, you need to go for an early morning jog tomorrow,' he said and smiled.

'Okay, thank you,' I said and hurriedly left for home. I needed to think.

Eleven

It all still did not make any sense to me. I didn't want to listen to Dr Karan and what he had said. I concluded that whatever he was saying was pretty useless to me. I decided to go back to Scotland and look for Aryan myself. It was not remotely possible for Aryan to not exist. I called up Rishika and told her what Dr Karan had just told me and how that did not make sense at all. To my surprise she asked me to look into its possibility.

'Aveera, it's possible that Dr Karan might be right. Maybe you are being too delusional. Think about it—Aryan has not contacted you till now. You don't have his number. What other explanation could there possibly be?' she asked.

'Rishika, I can't believe even you are saying this. Listen, I need to speak with my dad. I'll call you later,' I said and hung up on her.

He was a real person at least.

That same day, I decided to tell my parents.

'Dad, I need to talk to you please,' I told my dad, who was sitting in the living room.

'Tell me, Aveera?' he said, looking up at me with a smile.

'Dad, I need to go back to Scotland. I have to finish my studies,' I said, not hinting at the fact that I actually wanted to go and fit the pieces of the puzzles together, and to find out about what had really happened with Aryan.

'No, Aveera. How can you go to Scotland now? You have barely recovered from all this and you can't really go back until you are fully well,' he said firmly.

'I am feeling much better, dad. I just need to go there. I'll do well there. It will be a good change for me and I would really feel happy,' I tried to convince him.

'I need to discuss this with the doctor. Have you told your mom? This does not feel right though, Aveera,' he said, disappointed and worried about me. I didn't blame him. He had every reason to be concerned, especially considering what had happened and how I was behaving now.

'Okay, Dad. But this is important to me. I need to go back and figure things out. I have to finish my studies. I started it. It cannot be left unattended any longer,' I said. He wasn't aware of the whole Aryan issue and I wasn't going to tell him before I had understood it for myself.

He sighed and left the room.

I didn't understand what was going on. I knew for a fact that it was indeed not possible for Aryan to not exist. I distinctly remembered all the times I had spent with him. It wasn't humanely possible for him to not exist.

'Aveera, what is this I hear? You want to go back to Scotland?' my mom came running to my room a little later. It seemed like dad's conversation with mom had not gone as well as I had hoped.

'Yeah, Mom. I have already been in touch with the school. They have agreed to have me back. Plus, all my friends are there; they are going to be there with me throughout. You don't have to worry,' I said, trying to convince her.

'But Aveera, you have barely recovered. How can you go

back to the same place?'

'Why not? Staying here is good, but I feel like I am missing out on so much in life, Mom. I do not want that. I need to resume my studies and my life there. Maa, please?' I said, almost bursting into tears.

'Okay,' she sighed, giving in. 'As long as you promise to call us daily and not do anything stupid. Let me talk to your dad and we can figure something out.'

'Thank you, Mom,' I said and hugged her.

I had to go. My life, my Aryan, was there. I had to do something concrete with my life. I couldn't waste my time sitting here, working with my father. My friends were waiting there for me. How could I have forgotten that? And I knew for a fact that Aryan was waiting there for me.

I dialled Rishika instantly to tell her that I had to go. 'Aveera. All well?' she asked, sensing the urgency in my voice.

'Yeah. I am going back to Scotland,' I informed her.

'What? Are you mad? Why would you do that? Aveera, what are you even saying?' Thus came her responses, flooding me with questions and nagging me.

'All right, calm down,' I said and continued. 'I have to resume my studies, bro. I need to find Aryan—and talk to him. Everything you guys are saying does not make sense at all. It's not humanely possible for him to not exist. Dr Karan made some sense but now it does not make any sense any more. Please be a good friend and just help me out here,' I said.

'Aveera, I don't know why you are doing this to yourself. Think twice before you take this decision.'

'Look, I have thought it through, okay?'

'Aveera—'

'And as of now, I just want to go back to Scotland and I

need you to help me through this. Please? I need a friend. That's all,' I said. It was a genuine request more than anything else.

'Okay, whatever you say,' Rishika relented. 'But I'd still ask you to be careful. Because you are my friend and I do not want to see you hurt.'

'I know you don't,' I said, trying my best to tell her that I'd be okay. In my mind, I was just thinking about figuring things out. I knew the guy I loved existed and he was there, somewhere, waiting for me. All those trips with him, all those letters he wrote to me, they could not be unreal. I was determined to find him.

'Okay, Aveera. Have you finished your sessions with Dr Karan?' she asked.

'Yeah, I have finished them. He was very helpful, but I need to take up some things on my own,' I said, limiting what Dr Karan had said in the last session. It wasn't a complete lie, but I needed to go to Scotland as soon as I could. The doctor had indeed been very helpful, I was feeling better having spoken to him, but I couldn't believe what he had said. Going to Scotland was very important to me. It wasn't just about Aryan but also that I had to finish what I had started. I did not want to be left trailing behind my friends' successes.

'Now that you have made up your mind, Aveera, I just want to say that you should be careful. We do not want to lose our daughter yet again. We love you with all our hearts, so please, take care of yourself. If you want, we can come with you,' my mother said, coming into my room all teary-eyed.

'Mom, don't worry. I know you guys love me, I really really want you guys to know that I will be okay,' I said, and went to pack.

Rishika helped with everything and got me a ticket. I was

to fly out in three days and honestly, I felt very sick. There was a void inside me, an ache. It was a weird feeling and I did not know how to even put it into words. I knew I was going in search of myself—and in search of my love—but God almighty knows, I wasn't sure what was going to happen considering all the chaos I had been through.

But still, I needed to make sure that something good would happen in my career, and for that I had to finish my studies. I was lagging behind in my goals and aspirations.

As I was busy with my thoughts and the things I had to pack, my phone started to ring. I gathered my senses back and answered.

'Hi, Kabir.'

'Hi, Aveera. I heard that you are going back to Scotland. Are you sure?' he asked with concern in his voice. The truth was that I missed Kabir. I wanted to tell him that, but knowing how we had last spoken, I avoided saying anything dramatic.

'Yeah. It is important for me to go now. Nothing makes sense here and it will keep getting worse if I do not go,' I assured him.

'Yeah, I get that. I miss you bud. I really do. Come back soon and bring back the real Aveera,' he joked.

I laughed. 'I miss myself too, Kabir. I'll be back soon, to my favourite place, and then we shall plan a trip to Goa—all of us—where the sky merges with the water,' I said happily, hopefully.

'Sure. The most un-planned trip. Take care,' he said and hung up. Kabir had already cut the call. Our unspoken bond always bothered me, but now I just wanted it to be the way it used to be. I was not really sure where my life was headed.

As time passed, the panic attacks paid a visit once in a while but I seemed to be on a whole new mission. I was focused.

'All okay?' asked my mother. She had been hovering over me over the past couple of days, helping and concerned.

'I am good mom, everything is okay.'

'Oh okay,' she said. 'I'll leave you to your packing. Let me know in case you need anything,' she said and left. I resumed my packing and was almost done. I had to go meet Dr Karan the next day to thank him for all the help. I needed to seek the answers myself. For what I knew, what he had said was not possible at all. He was wrong about whatever he had said about Aryan not existing.

I slept fitfully, a lot of stress occupying my mind, and it was a tough night. I kept waking up in the middle of the night again and again. The breathing exercises he had taught me helped a little. It was probably anxiety, and the knowledge helped me get through the night. The next morning, I left for Dr Karan's house.

'Dr Karan?' I shouted at his window. His doorbell had not rung.

'Coming, coming,' I heard him from a distance. Something was wrong with his doorbell.

'You're early!' he said as he opened the door.

'Yeah, a little,' I said anxiously, biting my nails.

'All okay? Come in, come in,' he said, aware that something was up.

'Yeah, it's nothing actually,' I said, trying to be as calm as possible.

I went inside and got comfortable on a chair and had a glass of water before I told Dr Karan what I was planning on doing. 'So I have decided to go back to Scotland since none of you believe me.'

'What? Aveera—'

'Yes?'

'We all believe you…but right now, you need to believe us.'

'No, Doctor. It's impossible to believe what you have been claiming. How can a person I spent time with not exist?' I asked. I was furious about everything that had been confusing me.

'All right Aveera, we talked about it. You should know best. Just calm down and try to think straight,' he said, trying his best to make the situation a little better.

'Thank you, Dr Karan. I thank you for all the help. I am with you. I understand what you are saying, but I have to go and see for myself,' I said and got up, bidding goodbye in a hurry. All he did was shake his head in disappointment. I could see it in his eyes. But it was important for me to understand why everyone was saying what they were saying. I couldn't imagine having lived a lie.

I came back home that day restless. I was scared about what awaited me in Scotland. I was in touch with my Scotland friends but it wasn't like before. I didn't know if they'd accept me. I hoped they would. I wanted their help to complete my course and look for a decent job. And most importantly, I had to look for Aryan and see for myself what was real.

I was excited and nervous at the same time.

'Are you still sure about this?' my mother asked me over and over again.

And I kept answering the same way. 'Yes. Maa, don't worry.'

I later overheard my dad talking to my mother, saying that they needed to support me—no matter what. I had been through a lot, he said to her. I was glad for their support and slept well that night. I left for the airport the next day with my brother.

'Take care, idiot,' he said as he drove with me in the seat next to his.

'Yeah idiot,' I said with a smile.

My brother and I had always been the best of friends since childhood. When we had the occasion to talk, we had real conversations. But the occasions were rare as they came. It was that kind of a relationship that we shared.

'Are you sure you're going to talk it out with Aryan?' he asked, reassuring my faith that Aryan actually existed, and was actually waiting for me in Scotland. I felt that he was the only one who believed in me.

'Yeah, I believe in what we shared. Besides, it's just not him that I am going back to. I feel like I'm lagging behind here and missing out on so much that life has to offer. I am still young, but because of the accident, I feel like I've aged so much. I am fine mentally, completely. I know, I can feel it,' I said, but I wasn't sure really. I was trying to convince myself.

It's sometimes hard to even understand what one is going through. Was I recovering? Was I sad or just anxious? So many questions bothered me. I cannot really make sense of it all. For now, I felt that I was okay, that it was just anxiety that was bothering me. I was going back to Aryan—to seek answers, to ask him where he had been and to just catch up for the time we had lost. But everyone telling me that he, in fact, wasn't real, made it harder for me to decide how that was going to happen.

'Chal, don't worry about it,' my brother said, interrupting my thoughts. 'Go with a fresh mind and perspective and just make the most of your time there. You have another chance to live your dream. Not everyone is lucky enough to experience it, so don't waste this chance. And do not do anything stupid while you're there.' He gave me a wicked smile, as if he knew about everything.

'Obviously. Don't worry about it. I am fine and I have control over myself and my senses. Just chill,' I said and smiled, convincing him of my well-being.

'Hahaha! All right. Take care, baba. Your happiness matters the most to us,' he said. We then drove in silence for the rest of the journey. It was only when we reached the airport that my brother broke the silence and said, 'Listen Aveera, I just need you to know that we are here for you—no matter what. No matter what,' he said, emphasizing on it, as if he was conveying something important. 'Do not ever hesitate to reach out. Now go out there and live your dream. Love you, kid!' He gave me a quick hug.

'Love you,' I said and walked into the airport, tears rolling down my cheeks.

As I boarded the plane for Scotland, I couldn't help but think of the time when I had met Aryan on the plane. There was an announcement for him. An announcement for Aryan! How was that possible if he didn't exist?

Even now, I felt that I could hear his voice.

An hour into the flight, I got up and went to the back of the plane, where Aryan and I had had a conversation. I could smell him. I closed my eyes to take a moment to remember him. I wanted to let that feeling sink in.

'You all right, Ma'am?' the airhostess asked. She must have thought that I was having some issue breathing. I had been standing so still and quiet.

'Yeah. I am okay. Just enjoying the moment.' I told her. And then I asked, 'Ever been in love?' I don't have any idea why I uttered it.

'Sure, Ma'am,' she said, and gave me a strange look. She must have thought I was a rather weird person. I kept still, standing there. I only moved when our plane started to act up and an announcement was made for us to put the seatbelts back on. 'Ma'am, if you're done feeling in love, I request you to please take your seat,' the same airhostess said as I was walking towards my seat; as if she was mocking me.

People do not understand what another person might be feeling. It's a shame that she was trying to make fun of me. But I went back to my seat quietly. There was enough turbulence for me to feel like the plane was on a pockmarked road, flying on some pits, stones and pebbles. I wondered if this would be the end. As if enough had not already happened that year.

After almost forty minutes of that turbulence, we final got a signal to unfasten the seat belts and take it easy. It came as a relief. I distracted myself with a movie and the time went by.

Twelve

As I got out of the airport, a different kind of paranoia struck me. I felt like there was no air to breathe, and I gasped to catch a breath and not choke. Immediately outside, I sat down on a bench nearby and drank some water. I was so afraid.

But my sessions with Dr Karan had at the least helped me figure out certain ways in which I could cope. I took a deep breath after chugging the glass of water and repeated to myself out loud, 'It's going to be fine. It's going to be fine. You have got this.' I had learned this with him, a technique that would make me feel assured and motivated. It helped me deal better with situations.

Calmer now, I dialled Andrew's number. He was my go-to person in Scotland. He didn't pick up at first, but I got a call back the very next moment.

'Aveeeeraaaa, my darling, you're here! I missed you so much,' he crooned at me. He sounded really excited and I could hear it in his voice. He was supposed to come pick me up from the airport. But a project at his new office had come up and he couldn't make it. I was relieved to know that my friends had missed me.

A part of me had kept thinking about how I had missed out on so much. I feared that I had lost all my friends, that they had gotten used to being without me. I was scared about living alone in the hostel now. I would be without Andrew, Lance and Ally. They were all working now, and lived separately. I spoke with Ruchi, hoping to reconnect with her. She was really busy and her new job was really taking a toll on her, she said.

I booked an Uber and left for my hostel. Again, all the memories flashed by. I remembered the journey back from Iceland. I remembered I had Aryan with me then. I remembered everything. I remembered the accident.

At this thought, a sudden wave of nausea overcame me. I had gone into a coma, and so much had happened after that. I felt a little uneasy in the cab but I used my self-help tricks to calm myself down until I reached the hostel.

I stepped out and it felt new all over again. I felt like I would again meet Aryan in some bar. As I went back to my room, I could see new faces. The school was kind enough to give me my old room, 6B, and also to help with the entire process of finishing the degree I had begun to work for. I sat on my bed and heaved a sigh of relief. It felt comfortable—but only to a certain extent. There was a hidden anxiety to it.

I moved the curtains and saw the beautiful skyline. The sun had almost set. An innate happiness filled me as I looked up at the sky. I don't know why the sky and the water fills me with such hope. I always rest when I'm under a beautiful sky or near peaceful waters. Back when I used to be myself, that used to be the place for me. As I was lost in my thoughts, I was interrupted by a knock at my door. I wondered who it was. *Was it Aryan?*

It must be him! He was always there when I thought about him. He must have known that I had come back.

I rushed to get the door, unlocked it and saw a short girl

standing by herself, all smiles.

'Hi, you are Aveera, right?' she asked. She seemed like an Indian by nationality. I could discern that from her accent. But no one could have guessed where she was from based on how she looked.

'Yeah, I am Aveera. You are?' I asked, curious as to how she already knew about me.

'I am Sara. I stay in the next room. I heard about the accident that happened. In fact, everyone knows about it. I just wanted to say that if you need anything, I'm around,' she said kindly, smiled and left.

I stood there long after she had left, hanging by the door, wondering who all knew about me and what they knew.

Well, okay. I thought to myself and went in. Had I really thought it would be Aryan? I was too naïve to think that way. I called my parents and everyone back home and conveyed my safe arrival to them. It was mandatory, especially since the accident.

'Be safe, and study with all your heart,' my mother said.

'Yeah mommy, I will. Don't worry,' I assured her. She seemed partially convinced.

'Here, talk to your brother,' she said and handed the phone over to my brother, who joked as soon as he had the phone to his ear.

'How are you, Madam?' he asked.

'Haha! I am good. I've reached safely. Chilling in my room now,' I said. 'Tej, bro, where's dad? Let me talk to him too.'

'Hi beta, how are you?' the calm and composed voice of my dad soothed me. We hadn't really spoken much after I'd told him about my decision to return to Scotland. It was nice to hear him now.

'I am good, Dad. How are you? I will be happy and fine here,' I said.

'I am fine, Aveera. Whatever makes you happy, Aveera. Just be careful about everything,' he said.

'Yes, Dad,' I said. After which we said goodbye and I hung up.

I did not honestly know what I wanted to do or where I was going to start. I had thought that Aryan would have found me by now and we would have finally met. *He was always there whenever I wanted him, wasn't he?* I thought. I went to bed worried and dizzy. It was only in the morning that I opened my eyes and saw the heavy rain welcome me. I had five missed calls from Andrew.

'Shit!' I said out loud; I was supposed to meet Andrew last night, nearby, at the pub.

I immediately called him. He picked up and before he could say anything, I apologized. 'Sorry, so sorry, Andrew. I was so tired. I didn't know when my nap turned into a good night's sleep! I'm really sorry,' I said.

'It's okay! Breathe! I am glad you got a good night's sleep. I am at work now, but let's meet in the evening today?' he asked.

'Ah, you're such a sweetheart,' I said, relieved he wasn't angry. He was genuinely the most understanding person I had ever met. I was also supposed to catch up with Ally and Lance during the weekend. Scotland had already begun to make me feel okay.

'Beautiful,' I said, looking at the view outside. I rushed for my class. My professor would help me catch up on the syllabus, he had said. I had booked separate tutorials with the professors I knew, who were supportive enough to agree to the one-on-one sessions.

The classes went well, but as I wrapped up the sessions, I started getting that same old feeling. I felt an unrest, as if someone was choking me to death. I breathed hard. It was probably because I was going back to my hostel. It was the same place where Aryan and I had had our drunk conversation, and I still felt his touch, even though I was now in a far and distant place. I could feel him around me.

'Why aren't you here? Why?' I said out loud, scaring a girl behind me as I crossed the road. She immediately hurried past me. I rushed to my room and cried my heart out. I couldn't stop crying. That moment had felt so real. But it was real enough for me to consider what Dr Karan had said. It was *too* real. I called up Ruchi to see if she was free to meet me at that very moment but she disconnected the call. I dropped her a text asking her to call me as it was urgent. I waited for her reply while wiping off my tears.

I calmed myself down, softly speaking to myself. I heard my phone ring as I drew a breath. It was Andrew.

'Hey, we are on for today?' he asked.

'Yes. I'll see you in an hour,' I said, unable to control myself, and sobbing.

'You okay?' he asked.

'Yeah, its nothing. Let's meet and talk,' I said and hung up. I actually couldn't wait to meet Andrew and share my ordeals with him. He would comfort me. I got up and washed my face, ready to meet Andrew.

At the pub, I smiled from a distance as I saw Andrew waiting for me. 'Oh my god. I missed you so much. I love you so much,' I said as I neared him. I reached out and hugged Andrew.

'My baby. Missed you too!' he reciprocated. We sat down

and got ourselves a pint of beer each.

'What's been happening, Aveera?' he asked.

'Nothing, Andrew. You know everything that has happened so far. I am waiting for some answers—that's all. I don't know how to get past anything. You remember, how excited I was about Aryan, and now…everyone…including you, say that he does not exist. How is it possible? I fail to understand,' I said softly.

'Aveera, I checked. I got the CCTV footage and there was no one there except for you. You need to accept this!' he exclaimed.

'I need to see for myself to believe it. Tomorrow I am going to the admissions office to check for Aryan's records,' I said.

'Fine, Aveera. Maybe then you will believe it. But don't worry, all this will be over soon. Don't get so worked up,' he said. He was the same, always being the one to handle a situation in the calmest way possible.

'Yeah, hopefully, Andrew. Thank you for being there. I know I have been stuck for a long time and I am sorry for that,' I said.

'Are you mad? I am your friend, and that's what friends are for,' he said and picked up his beer and said happily, 'Cheers!' I smiled and clinked glasses with him.

'So, when is the wedding?' I asked Andrew with a wink.

'Well, we both are so busy. We have not been able to come to a consensus. It will most likely be held sometime next year. March maybe?'

'That's great! Six months!' I was happy for them. 'Remember, I told you about how Aryan proposed?' I said, and at that moment, I suddenly thought of the ring.

'Where's the ring? Where's my ring that he gave me?' I suddenly got up in a panic, unable to remember where it was. Had I lost it during the accident? Or after?

'Aveera! Aveera! Calm down. Have some water,' Andrew came

and rubbed my shoulder. He continued, 'Look my dear, you need to stop telling yourself that he exists. There never was a ring. We never saw one, and we were with you the whole time.'

I didn't say a thing. I just kept thinking that Andrew might be right. There might never have been a ring after all. But I had to make sure. This wasn't how I had imagined things would be.

'Look, Aveera, let's go. Okay? You need to calm down and think the whole thing through,' he said.

'Go where, Andrew?' I asked, looking at the ground.

'The hostel? Go and check with the admissions office—or whatever you have planned. See it for yourself,' he said.

'Of course, I will,' I replied. I felt tired and weak, I didn't want this.

'Don't get angry with me, Aveera. I'm trying to help here, nothing else,' Andrew said, disappointed. It was obvious on his face.

'I know, I know. I am sorry, I really am. I did not mean to panic. I just don't know how to make you understand what's in my mind. It's definitely not good,' I replied.

'Look, I really want to help you out, Aveera. I want things to be as smooth as possible for you, but the only one who can actually help you is you. No one else. Just be careful okay?' he said.

'Yeah,' I replied, finishing the beer in a gulp. 'Cool, I'll better get going. I have classes in the morning and then I am going to the admissions office. And weirdly enough, Ruchi is not talking to me. Even Ally hasn't confimed if she will meet me over the weekend.'

'Really? Well, that's weird,' he said.

'Yeah, they say they've been busy but I don't understand,' I said. 'Anyway, thank you so much for meeting me, Andrew.

I'll see you soon.' I hugged him as we both got up to leave.

I reached my hostel and I couldn't hold back my tears as I walked into my room. I didn't know what the right time would be to give up on this search. Nothing seemed to make sense. The engagement ring was lost, or it didn't exist. It didn't make sense. I called Ruchi.

'Hey,' she said.

'Hey, are you busy?'

'Not really, what's up?'

'Why won't you meet me, Ruchi? It's been a while. I have been trying to reach out to you since I was in India. I even called you today and texted but you didn't reply. What is the matter?' I asked. I was concerned. I didn't want to lose a friend.

'Dude, you've got to stop this Aryan shit. Okay? It's driving us crazy. Andrew and I both have tried so hard to make you understand that he does not exist. It's enough. It's time to stop. I honestly do not want you to go through this again. Start a new life and make your peace with things now,' she said, all in one go.

'Whoa…slow down Ruchi. I am sorry. I didn't want to bring this into your life. I really am sorry. I won't meet you, sorry,' I said. I heard her breathing on the other end.

'Aveera—' she began. But I hung up.

I felt horrible. Maybe she was right. This had been going on for too long. I should have stopped. But I didn't understand how I could. I had spent a considerable time with Aryan and no one believed that. It hurt when Ruchi talked to me like that. Was I causing everyone pain? With these thoughts I went to bed, crying myself to sleep.

I went to class the next morning, my eyes puffy. No one said anything. After the classes ended, I went straight to the admissions office to check for someone named Aryan.

'Yeah—Aryan—that's all I know. He was doing his PhD here,' I told the lady at the admissions office. I was trying my best to not appear distraught. She was helping me out with the entire thing.

'Wait a minute, let me check for you,' she said. She started looking through her computer, typing furiously. It had been hard to convince her and give me the details. Even though Andrew and Lance had already helped once and had checked, I didn't believe them.

'Umm…Aveera, is that right?' she asked, looking up at me.

'Yeah,' I responded, hopeful.

'Unfortunately, the server is down right now. Could you come back later in the evening? There seems some problem in the back end now,' she said, as kindly as possible.

I was worried. But I agreed to come back. I hope she knew how important it was for me to check. I went back to my hostel room. I had begun to feel lonely again. It had again begun to feel as if I was growing crazier—day by day. To distract myself, I started looking at the possibilities of a part-time job. I hoped it would help me get rid of everything that was on my mind.

That evening I did not go to the admissions office. Students were protesting against the hike in the fees. A few days passed, and I decided to focus on my classes and on finishing up my course.

I had applied for a few jobs and soon I heard back from a cosmetic brand. They wanted to give me an opportunity in their customer care section. I was delighted. After such a long wait, I would finally start working. I kept busy after that. All my time was spent in classes, after which I would go to work.

One day at work, I was caught up in thought when I heard a voice behind me. 'Aveera, Aveera? What are you doing?'

It was one of my colleagues at the cosmetics store. I hadn't realized it, but there were about six customers in the queue for cash checkout. I was lost in thought; I had been thinking about Aryan.

'I am sorry. I am sorry, really,' I said and immediately got back to work.

After we were done with the day, the manager called me aside. 'Aveera, this has happened a lot of times now. We can have an amicable process of separation, but we do not want careless people working here.'

'I am sorry. This won't happen again, please,' I said. I did not want to leave.

'Careful,' she said and left. I was glad that she had let me off the hook this time around. As I heaved a sigh of relief, I noticed Sara, my flatmate. She was wearing our work uniform.

'Hey, do you work here?' she asked, excited. I nodded.

'Oh great! Now we can work together and commute together. How exciting!' she said.

It didn't amuse me at all. We weren't friends and I didn't know why she was happy about this. 'Sure,' I said.

That day, we both returned to the hostel together.

'Listen, I kind of know what happened to you—all your mental breakdowns,' she said hesitantly as we walked.

'What?' I said. I was shocked.

'I just know,' she said.

'This is weird. You don't even know me.' I was angry.

'Almost everyone knows you here. Your friends told everyone everything.'

I was shocked to hear that. Why would my friends tell

everyone what had happened? This was beyond my wildest imagination.

'Okay,' I said in a huff, I didn't say anything further. I went straight to my room and didn't look at her. I called Andrew immediately.

'Andrew, did you guys tell everyone at this hostel about my situation?' I demanded.

'What? No! Why would we do that? Are you mad?'

'I just heard from someone. She seemed to know almost everything.'

'Aveera, everyone knows about your accident…but nothing beyond that. Nothing about Aryan for sure,' he explained.

'Okay,' I said in disbelief and hung up. All of this had shocked me. I honestly had no idea what had to be done. But it was what it was. There was nothing I could have done about people knowing. Days passed and I had no clarity, nothing that could have held any possible meaning for me. It was getting more complicated instead.

Sara, on the other hand, was trying to be extremely helpful when I next met her.

'Hey. Shh, shh. Please, let's go. Let's go out,' Sara took me by my arm one day. She had come in when she heard me crying in my room. 'You have got to feel okay now, Aveera,' she said.

'Yeah,' I said, thanking her for taking care of me. While Ruchi and Ally weren't meeting me, Sara, despite being a stranger, seemed to care. Back home, my friends felt troubled and even in Scotland, everyone seemed upset about the Aryan thing. Maybe it was time to stop thinking about it. I felt like I had lost all my friends because of my obsession over this whole thing.

But at the same time. I was improving each day. At least I was trying to. Work had gotten easier to bear and I made fewer mistakes. I called my parents often and I always told them that I was doing quite well.

'Yeah Maa, trust me,' I would tell her on the phone. But immediately after I would hang up, I would shed tears. Even though I still didn't believe that Aryan didn't exist, I was learning to live without him. I was focusing more on myself— my education, my work.

One night, I dreamt of Aryan. We were enjoying ourselves in Paris. I immediately got up when I remembered that Aryan had asked me to book his ticket for him. I remembered booking his ticket along with mine. I checked my email to look for the ticket. I felt a little hopeful. I opened my email only to find that there was only one ticket, and it was in my name. I had travelled to Paris alone, and not with him. I closed my eyes and felt his touch on my lips as we were sitting right in front of the Eiffel Tower. His scent was so refreshing, his touch felt like dewdrops mildly falling on the grass. But my mind went blank right away. Aryan wasn't there now. It was just me, sitting with my eyes closed, all by myself in front of the Eiffel Tower. I was breathing the fresh air. I could only see myself.

Startled, I opened my eyes. Had it just been me then? Aryan hadn't been there after all. It seemed like I could picture what had happened there. Both the images were so clear. I prayed to God and went back to sleep.

I did not talk about this incident to anyone and tried my best to stay calm. As the days passed, my studies were successful and my days at work were smooth, and I remembered so much.

A few days during the weeks that passed, I still missed Aryan. But I thought more about myself. I was proud of how I was trying to keep myself together. I did not try to reach out to my friends any more. I had given them a hard time and it was my duty to amend things.

'Let's go, Aveera?' Sara asked one day as we were getting late for work. I nodded and smiled at her, after which we both went to work.

'Listen, I think I saw your Aryan today,' she said while we were walking.

'Huh?' I stopped and looked at her. I was surprised.

'I am sorry. I shouldn't have mentioned this, I think. But I saw a guy a few times; he was looking at you. It was both creepy but loving at the same time. Could that be Aryan?' she asked.

'Really? Where? Can you show me?' I asked. I was excited. I was hopeful. I would finally have the answers I so desired.

'Sure, I will. Today,' she said with a smile.

I don't know who she had seen but his name had lit up my soul. I waited as I worked, thinking about Aryan the entire time.

'Did you see him yet?' I asked, over and over again. Each time she would say, 'Not yet.'

And I would return to my disappointment. As we ended our day at work, we both left for the hostel. She came with me to my room. She held my hand kindly and took me to the washroom. I had a big mirror up in the washroom.

'What are you doing, Sara?' I asked her.

'Showing you Aryan,' she said.

'What? Where?' I asked.

'Look,' she said. She pointed to my image in the mirror and as I was staring at myself, she turned around and left.

I stood there, still looking at myself. Aryan was me? What?

I found myself going to a cupboard and opening it. There were small boxes with locks inside it. I remembered Aryan had given me love letters. I opened the boxes. It had the letters. I started to read them, one by one.

Dear Aveera,

Remember, you are worthy of love. You are beautiful, inside and out. You have so much love inside you, the entire world around you could share it if they wanted. But before all, love yourself. You are awesome. You are a badass. Stop running away from things. Let things sink in, and take the privilege of feeling things. You are a human being. Allow yourself to feel all your emotions and allow yourself to be loved and to love others. What are you scared of? Love? Life? Career? What do you fear of missing out on? Each second of your life passes in the blink of an eye. You have enough time in this life, but not enough time to live. Live each second of your life. Be grateful for being alive. I love you, Aveera. All the scars of the past have only made you stronger. You are so capable of loving yourself that when you allow someone else to love you, it will only add to the love you already have in your life. Remember, without that you are still complete. Your life is going to turn out beautiful. You will succeed. You are blessed. I guess I'm falling harder for you each day. Just keep being kind to people, places and things. Life will fall into place. I love you—a lot!

Love

Tears started to roll as I read the note. Not because of what was written, but because I recognized who had written it. It was my handwriting. All the letters had my handwriting in them, they were written to me by my own hand. Aryan had never existed after all. I had been making myself happy all this while. No one else. Dr Karan's words made sense. Everything made sense. I didn't know why it had happened.

I immediately went to Sara's room, only to find out that she was gone. She was nowhere to be found. I rushed downstairs to the hostel staff to ask about her.

'Sara?' they asked.

'Yeah, Sara. Room 6A?' I enquired.

'I am sorry, Miss, but that room is empty,' she said.

'What?' I was shocked.

What was happening? I took a brief moment to calm myself down. I remembered the sky and the water. My place for peace. I remembered I dreamt of a girl named Sara and then, it began to make sense. I rushed towards the beach in an Uber. There were feelings of immense peace and unrest at the same time. Trillions of untouched emotions and senses were coming to the surface. I reached the beach and at the sight of the water, I heaved a sigh of relief.

'Thank you so much. You're the best,' I told the driver. He gave me a perplexed look. He had brought me where I wanted to be in time and I just wanted to thank him out loud.

'You're welcome,' he said and shook his head in amusement. He must have been confused about my over-enthusiastic tone.

I rushed towards the beach as the car drove away, onto the road not taken. Or so I thought, at that moment. I removed my footwear and put it aside, and started to walk towards the sea. To hold that moment close, I shut my eyes and then opened them again to look at the beautiful sky. The setting sun made it even more beautiful.

'To the skies and the waters,' I said to myself.

It started to drizzle. Sara was me. Even Aryan had been me all along. All these people were just a part of my own being and my imagination, there to teach me a lesson about life. If *you* get yourself into a pit, *you* get yourself out of it. It made sense.

I suddenly felt at peace. I felt good. It was all good. I walked towards the water and kept immersing my toes in the sand and sea as the sun sets...

I saw Sara standing there. My own reflection.

'Sara!' I cried out.

'Aveera, come,' she and I said, and I, laughing and giggling all by myself, ran towards the water.

Epilogue

Mental health is a serious problem that affects almost everyone around the world. Common to it is the destruction of one's self-esteem and self-worth. Suddenly, those who suffer start losing hope; everyone and everything seems useless. The ocean of tears and waves of thought flood us and it seems like the end of the world. However, we forget that even the wave finds the shore. Even in the dark night, the moon never refuses to come out and shine. After a dark night, comes a beautiful sun. You are a beautiful creature on this planet and nothing, nothing at all, is more important than your love for yourself. Remember, someone out there loves you and that is you. Look in the mirror and say to yourself—You are awesome! You are valued! You are loved!

Society has created many barriers to prevent the resolution of issues of mental health. But remember, it is okay to seek help, to reach out to people and talk to them. Even not feeling okay is OKAY, but what's not okay is to think that it's the end of the world!

You are a human being, but you are also a fighter. After all the species that have come and gone, after all these generations, you are alive and breathing. It is not fair to put yourself under the microscope and feel worthless because somebody, somewhere, has said so. You are beautiful. I love you.

Acknowledgments

'Agar chhoti si har ek nehar sagar ban bhi jaaye…
koi tinka lekar dhundh hi lenge hum…kinaare'

I was listening to this song at work when I suddenly found myself opening my laptop to write. I did not know what I was about to write, or what I had already set to words, but I just kept typing. Sitting at WeWork, an incredible co-working space, I finally got out of my writer's block. And the best part was that I was smiling while I wrote, caught up in my imagination.

This novel is an attempt to make us love ourselves a little more.

I'm eternally grateful to the people who have helped me throughout this journey. First, I would like to thank the Almighty God for constantly blessing me and for guiding me through the good and the bad times. Thank you, friend!

Mannat, thank you for constantly rooting for me while I was writing this novel. I'm blessed to have a friend like you.

My other friends, thank you for always being so *so* supportive. You know who you are.

My heartfelt gratitude to my family for always sticking around. Mom, Dad, Chachu, Maasi, Vaddi Maa, Papa, Bua, Fufar ji—thank you so much!

My best people in this world—Sohaj Veerji, Sukhan, Sukrat, Simran, Kanwal Bhabhi, Vishav Veerji, Supreet and Seerat—thank you, my loves, for never letting me feel for a second that I was alone. Thank you for pushing me to write this novel and for always supporting me. I love you with all my heart.

Finally, my sincere thanks to the entire team of Rupa Publications for bringing this novel to life and for helping me throughout the publication process!